THE EMPEROR'S TWIN

THE EMPEROR'S TWIN

HONEY WATSON

Talos Press books may be purchased in bulk at special discounts for sales promotion, corporate gifts, fund-raising, or educational purposes. Special editions can also be created to specifications. For details, contact the Special Sales Department, Talos Press, 307 West 36th Street, 11th Floor, New York, NY 10018 or info@skyhorsepublishing.com.

Talos Press is an imprint of Skyhorse Publishing, Inc.®, a Delaware corporation.

Visit our website at www.skyhorsepublishing.com.
Please follow our publisher Tony Lyons on Instagram @tonylyonsisuncertain

10 9 8 7 6 5 4 3 2 1

Library of Congress Cataloging-in-Publication Data is available on file.

Cover design: Kai Texel
Cover photo: Getty Images

Print ISBN: 978-1-945863-89-9
Ebook ISBN: 978-1-945863-90-5

Printed in the United States of America

for James

PART I

The Emperor's Twin

1

A stolen apartment, the thief inside.

Hexagonal tiles across a vaulted ceiling in coral shades of pink and green. Therapeutic eruptions from the belly of an enormous bathtub. The scene might have been peaceful in an affectedly mid-century sort of way had Ming not been inhabiting it for so long. Months, but to her it felt much longer.

Stained towels, broken tile, strangers' clothing. Evidence of violences myriad but only half-enjoyed—Ming's attempts to alleviate her boredom in confinement.

The wax of rose petals, pinched between her fingers. The stench of disinfectant.

A mechanical arachnid whirled beside her left ear. It cared for her with mindless affection, releasing antibacterial love into the air whenever it sensed the need. It did so. Her tongue emerged through the ragged decay of her mouth to taste it. Acrid. An expression of vacant loss somewhere beneath her damaged flesh.

"Come here," Ming commanded, her voice soft with pain. One of her experiments in self-mutilation near destroyed her tongue but the captured ship was full of people who could fix it for her whether they liked it or not. "I'm sick of having to press this button to talk to you."

There was nobody else in the room, the door was closed. She was speaking to the apartment's former owner, a hostage lightly guarded in the room beyond.

Sound came from a system at the bathtub's edge. A low voice, enunciating slowly, as if its owner was afraid to talk.

"I don't think I'm allowed," the voice said.

"Allowed?" she answered, repeating the distasteful word for to whom did the prisoner think they answered if not to her. She rose, changed her mind, sank back into the grime. She had been angry for so long that she could no longer be bothered to act the part. "Speaker," she said, the prisoner's name, "Speaker, get in here."

The door opened, revealing Speaker's face. Thin, sleepless, with long lank hair which they had tried to braid despite everything. Unrecognizable from the adorned politician they had been before their capture. "Should the guards come in, too?"

"No. Send them away. You're not going to hurt me."

Ming was right. It was not that Speaker didn't fantasize about killing her, dreamed of the thrill as they fixed their hands around her throat, held her down, watched her face turn Picasso when she struggled and thrashed beneath the water's distorting surface—revenge for the Crysthian Empire. But though Speaker's fear of death had long since faded, they still feared pain. The pain that would punish them for Ming's destruction was painful even to imagine. She was not the sole villain. The other one, her general and coconspirator, was possibly even worse.

The other one spent the majority of his time outside the safety of Speaker's apartment, battling in the war zone which he and Ming had made of the palatial ship to which it belonged. But his enemy was no longer Crysth, rather the army of foul things which he and Ming brought into the Zetland when they invaded the Empire. Grounded and infested, the Zetland was becoming home to an uneasy truce between conqueror and conquered as they united to restore order.

Ming heard complaints through the crack in the door, guards protesting their dismissal. She switched languages from her native Crysthian to the guards' Apechi. She told them to stay where they were. They grumbled a "Yes, Ming" before letting Speaker into the bathroom without them.

Ming is not her given name, it is her surname. Her given name is Wilhelmina but she will not answer to it—a habit begun when she was just a teenager. The peculiarity of her insistence on being "Ming" even then stemmed in large part from the fact that surnames are such a rarity in Crysth. They signal descendance from a few dozen prominent families but little else, having been divorced from any meaning they once had when they were plucked from the Earth era like lost works of art. Crysthian academics and social commentators had flagged the reappearance of surnames as a sign of their empire's decline—calling it a meaningless aesthetic decadence from the self-appointed ruling class. They may have been right. The empire has fallen and the architect of its destruction was Ming, but this would likely be of little comfort to them.

"Ah, I . . . I would like to bring in my chair, please. I want somewhere to put all my papers. It's so dirty in here," Speaker said.

Ming peered over the side of the tub, observing the fetid swamp she had made of the room as if this were news to her. She waved her hand in a *do what you like* fashion.

"Thank you."

Speaker fumbled with the silk legs of their pajamas. It was their last clean pair. They tried to fold the fabric away from the floor. Sweat, soap, semen, piss, blood. Other stuff. Speaker's heavy ringed eyes landed on their slippers. There was no hope for saving those without going barefoot, which would be unthinkable. They began to drag their least favorite chaise longue into the room.

As Speaker fussed into position Ming said, "Open some wine, pour us both a glass."

Speaker almost turned to face her in surprise. There had been no such thing as wine in Speaker's life since Apech took over the Zetland.

Speaker padded damply to the bar at the room's edge, a long tile recess built to their specifications back when they were the emperor's steward rather than a sad hostage. Speaker had spent countless evenings watching old films on the projector wall beyond the bathtub, but Ming never touched it. She did not care about anything other than her goal.

The former steward looked over their wines. They weren't sure whether red or sparkling was a more appropriate choice for the traitor-monster-usurper-devil in the tub. Surely a bubble bath calls for sparkling. They chose red as an act of rebellion.

A corkscrew trembled in their palm. How pretentious the little tool was, how preciously old-fashioned. But it was sharp. Speaker considered murder again. Their fingers tightened around the corkscrew's wooden head, steadying the spiral point as it angled downward. They sighed.

A sound of glass on porcelain as Speaker placed Ming's wine gently beside her.

"You used to drink a lot, didn't you?" Ming asked, rhetorically. "I said pour us both a glass. Perhaps you'll be more interesting if you're drunk."

Speaker had been recounting Crysth's final moments to Ming ever since she brought the empire to a standstill. She was searching for a clue in the story, something that might allow her to regain power over the force she had used to invade her former home. Apech is a theocracy, its people worship the weird magic that runs in their veins but they cannot control it; they do not even know what it really is. They think of it as a god, something to revere and persuade. It doesn't care.

Ming thinks that it is listening to her, that something in Speaker's memory will reveal the god's motives. Despite being Crysthian she worships the Apechi magic more zealously than any Apechi native and therein lies her misery. The god will not give her its blessing—it has given it to Speaker instead. Nobody knows why. Ming has convinced herself that one day the god will love her back.

"Alcohol certainly has the capacity to provide one with a greater self-introspective insight than one is afforded without," Speaker said.

Ming rolled her eyes. She had tried to torture the dead emperor's twin out of the habit of annoying her but nothing seemed to work. "Just have a drink, Speaker. Fuck."

Speaker obeyed. They sat on the chaise longue beside their notes, a selection of papers and tablets which they had begun to think of as their "debut auto-fictional endeavor" in the hopes that self-delusion might improve their psychological condition. "Where shall I begin this time?"

"From the beginning," she said. "No! I can't listen to all that miserable eulogizing about Juniper again. Start at the decision to consult Avon Stal."

Speaker looked for the relevant pages.

"And don't just read. Think about it, don't just tell me what you were doing, tell me why you were doing it. Everything. Every thought. It's in there somewhere."

As Speaker searched for the right page, they realized that Ming was whispering to herself. They listened.

It's in there somewhere. It's in there somewhere. It's in there somewhere . . .

2

So . . . that will have been a week after you killed Juniper.

I'm still going to have to talk about her death, if only to set the scene. I simply must. Atmosphere is crucial, nothing will make sense to a listener who does not understand that we had all gone mad. It was the apocalypse. An emperor of Crysth had been assassinated by an alien god in our capital city. It feels unreal even now; it was impossible. We didn't even know that Apech was a real threat to us before then. Juniper exploded before our eyes. She erupted into pieces of bone.

Pardon me? Well, I wish I had *not* been there to see it. It was disgusting.

But I digress.

It was the apocalypse. We only had three emperors left and nothing surprised us anymore. That's what my hypothetical audience—in this case just you, I suppose—needs to understand. We could not react appropriately to anything because everything was already the worst thing that had ever happened. We were "on the run." Nobody could believe what was happening to us and so we all simply went along with it. Even when "it," in retrospect, was the stupidest series of decisions you've ever heard in your life.

Juniper's death seemed huge, all encompassing, but it was just the first domino. I know, poor metaphor. I'm working on it. What I mean to say is that the first event in this series was so large that when the techs warned us that a second one was coming, we just ignored them. They were telling us that the machines weren't responding correctly to their input, and we were wondering why the hell they were bothering us with such nonsense. Just troubleshoot, we said. Hilarious really. The god of Apech was in our walls, in our ships, in our doors. It was everywhere. The moment of realization was . . . I don't know. Like suddenly realizing you've mistaken a stranger's house for your own. We couldn't troubleshoot shit because your god had converted our entire network to its cause. There was nobody with the capacity to imagine that something so grotesque could happen. It was so perfect an invasion that if we weren't the victims then I might admire you and Apech for having done it.

This is what we get, I admit, for powering our tech through what I must now understand as slavery. The "demons" were sentient! I didn't know. I swear I didn't know. I thought it was just another silly word like "technomancer" or even "god." Designed to stop people from looking into how it all really works rather than actually describe the thing itself. Once your god's virus had sneaked into their minds it was already over for us. They were turned against us overnight and we didn't notice. Nobody had the intellectual creativity to notice.

Another contributing factor to the whole chaos milieu—milieu of chaos—was that the palace seemed safe. It's off the grid of course, designed to detach from the capital planet if we needed to escape but that had never been done before. It's named after a lifeboat you know, that's where "Zetland" comes from. One of those facts that everybody learns so everybody forgets. It's almost romantic—refugees in our own home.

Everything was so awful but also very normal. Sleeping in our own beds, brushing our teeth, eating breakfast. Fleeing the occupied, fallen capital through empty space. Low-fat latte, extra foam.

Not that I would ever order such a thing myself. Just an example of what someone might.

*

Everybody was arguing that day, which was somewhat comforting. A little touch of normality. Juniper's empty throne still loomed, but the other three emperors were bickering enough that her absence didn't swallow the place.

"As the Military emperor," Vard was saying, "my suggestions should be given priority. This is war! It is not the time for philosophy."

"It is exactly that attitude," Daksha, the Ethicist emperor, was saying back, "that is always leading your generals into my courts with innocent blood on their hands!" Low blow. The argument wasn't just contained between the two emperors. The rest of the Military and Ethicist factions behind them were yelling at each other too. Totally incoherent but necessary, you can't let your faction's emperor argue without tossing in a good jeer. "It is also that attitude which got us here in the first place!"

"And what do you mean by that?" You could tell that Vard was angry. Was always interesting to watch him lose his cool, purely because he was very cool. There's something about allowing oneself to age that makes a person seem very self-assured, I think. Who else do you ever see with a receding hairline? So chic.

"I mean that if Military hadn't hidden from the rest of us that the things powering our machinery were actual living sentient beings then we wouldn't have allowed their use! Apech would never have been able to attack us like this!" Daksha hissed.

Vard scowled, which he could do very effectively with all that forehead. "If you truly believe that this is Military's fault then let Military take responsibility for fixing it."

I was just standing behind my brother's throne hoping for the best.

"May I remind you all," said my brother, and everyone always stopped to listen to him because his voice was so loud that you didn't really have a choice, "that we are dealing with an unnatural enemy. The technomancers should be better represented in this debate."

The techs looked like they disagreed. One of them said, "It is not an unnatural enemy we're up against with Apech, it is a so-called 'deity.' We aren't the deity people, we're the tech guys."

"Yes," called Vard, "and the 'deity people' are all dead! Which I once again assert leaves myself and the Military faction in command of this situation."

Military cheered. The Ethicists started shouting at them again.

Rhododendron had his head in his hands. It can't have been pleasant for him, holding the deciding vote between Military and Ethicist. Everyone went quiet again when he said, "Vard. Perhaps you could tell us your plan? Then at least we know what we're agreeing to."

We—by which I mean myself and the rest of the Reds—gave Rhododendron a round of sensible applause. Well, I say sensible applause but of course most of our faction have those nasty prosthetic hands which sound absolutely disgusting when they're touched together so applause was actually a form of psychological torture.

"Oh, stop that!" Daksha snapped at us, and she clicked her tongue in an imitation of the stone-sound the fake hands make to show us what she meant. "It's a foul noise and don't act like you don't know that you're doing it. I actually agree with you, Rhododendron."

Vard said, "Well my plan's no secret! I want to take us to general Avon Stal, who has proven through decades of service that she is our expert on supernatural warfare."

The Ethicist faction started yelling then quietened down when they realized that their emperor hadn't reacted yet. They watched her, waiting to see what they were supposed to think.

"That would usually be a good idea." Daksha began, slowly, feeling out her words. "But. This Apechi deity we are up against has infested our ships, our computers, the whole grid! That's everything other than the palace. Its virus will have contaminated her warship, too. Moreover, this deity seems to be our only real problem. We should just find the Apechi agent who is controlling it and kill them."

"We can't do that," said one of the techs. "Sorry, emperors. Like I said, deimancer ring's gone so everyone who could have done the god-finding stuff is dead. Bastards got 'em when they got Juniper. But Daksha's point about the virus still stands. Avon's ship will be compromised."

Vard shook his head. "Look. I didn't want to say this publicly." Congress went quiet when he said that, who doesn't love a secret? "But Avon Stal's ship is not on the grid. It is removed, like the Zetland."

"What!" Daksha yelled, standing up so that the light shone over her suit in a really beautiful way. She always had these perfect three-piece ensembles. I love the Ethicist colors, almost white but for threads of pink which shift it into a gleaming pearl. Her shoes too, a fabulous collection, don't think I've ever seen her in flats—Pardon me? You said I should say everything that comes to me and I—yes, yes. Sorry.

Naturally, she and her Ethicists were furious. The demons were for surveillance as much as power, nobody should be able to just remove a ship from the grid.

"General Avon Stal is the most experienced and competent commander the Crysthian empire has ever seen." said Vard. "She has spent her whole life fighting both physical and unnatural entities on our behalf! She needed the greater speed which removal from the grid afforded her. And thank goodness for that! Now we have a warship which this Apechi deity can't get into! We have hope!"

"Sorry, sorry," interrupted one of the techs. He wasn't saying "sorry" like he was apologizing he was saying "sorry" like he had been direly affronted. "How did she do that? There is no way to alter the grid without us knowing." He tapped his metal jaw, which the techs get when they reach the highest rank. It allows them to talk directly to the machines, apparently. Hideous.

"Exactly." was what Vard replied. "With all due respect . . . This invasion is mainly a problem with the grid. Apech seems to have no weapon other than its so-called deity. Avon Stal knows ways to manipulate the grid that our Zetland techs do not."

"Do we know that?" asked Rhododendron. "About Apech's potential weaponry, I mean. Are we certain—do we truly know that these Apechi people have nothing other than this alleged god's magic to hit us with?"

"We don't know much about them at all. Tiny planet, recent discovery." The tech was reading something nobody else could see while he was talking, eyes scanning left to right. "The planet was flagged because it looked like there was something unnatural going on, relatively weak. They must have really good control over the thing if it is a god because they managed to hide it from us until now. Would've nuked the place had we known it was there, obviously."

Vard himself had been nodding the whole time, looking over at Daksha with a sort of pleading expression. A bit pathetic but I suppose he did love her. He said, "See? Our priority needs to be figuring out what Apech's magic—or its deity—actually *is*. Avon Stal does that kind of thing all the time."

"Alright," Rhododendron said, "the Red faction agrees with Vard. Red and Military are in accord."

We applauded, of course. It's nice to know that one agrees.

Daksha was still mad. In retrospect I realize she must have thought this new revelation about the unauthorized grid removal made Avon Stal seem even less trustworthy than before. She said, "What about the Green faction?"

Vard got upset again about that. He said, "Why would we—see this is what I mean! The Green faction are architects, bankers! And their emperor is dead! What does it matter what they think about how we should go to war? Mine is the only relevant opinion in this room!"

The Greens roared behind Juniper's empty throne.

The Green steward cleared his throat and said, "Shall I represent Juniper, for the sake of this conversation?"

"May as well." Rhododendron grumbled.

"Yes, Cull. You may as well." Vard grumbled even harder.

Cull stepped forward away from the rest of the faction. "As much as it pains me to say this considering Vard's stated disregard for my input, I agree with him that we had better seek the advice of Avon Stal."

I was annoyed by that. I'm a steward too, nobody's ever asked me my opinion in congress. But Cull was so interesting, so I was also quite thrilled. He looked at me once he had spoken. I wish I knew what my expression had been doing. What did I convey? Awe, envy? He did not look at me again.

Vard said, "General Avon Stal should be happy to see us."

"What?" Rhododendron asked, "we're going to physically retrieve her? Isn't she still fighting all those witches? Shouldn't we be in hiding?" That probably would have sounded cowardly from anyone else, but Rhododendron was so huge that he could get away with saying things like that. His mere existence gave everyone else an excuse to hide behind him.

"I do not trust long-distance comms right now." replied Vard. "And she is not fighting, she already won. She is on the planet Hecubah overseeing its formal integration into our empire, she is probably bored and will be glad for another fight." Perverse.

"Well I hope you're prepared to go down to Hecubah to fetch her yourselves. I am having no part in this." said Daksha. Wish *I* could've had no part in this.

Rhododendron turned to look at me. He ignored my negative mouthings and said, "Speaker will go."

"Thank you, Speaker," said Daksha. At least she was polite to me. Nobody else was ever polite to me, and now look where they are.

Cull cleared his throat again, "I would like to volunteer myself, also. It's time for me to take up my responsibilities as leader of the Green faction."

Gods. Why? Why did he volunteer himself?

We crowned him as the Green emperor not long after that. Just a few days, I think. Most mediocre party I've ever been to. Suppose it would have been distasteful to have a proper celebration, his predecessor having recently exploded and all.

Why did he volunteer himself? He didn't speak the local language or anything.

Did he just want to go to see the magic planet? Is that kind of thing fun? Do people like that? I don't know.

Anyway. We crowned Cull as the Green emperor and despite the party's mediocrity we did all start to feel hope. We had a plan. We were on our way.

We thought that Avon Stal was going to save us. I still think she could have.

3

One of the details I remember about the time we spent on our way to Hecubah is that Daksha and Vard were openly in love. The palace mood was always lighter when they were together, although it could be irritating at times. Not Daksha and Vard themselves, but the rest of the Ethicists and Military. They would start flirting with each other all the time like horrible incestuous siblings. You wouldn't think they'd get along, seeing as it's always Ethicists charging Militaries with crimes against humanity etcetera. Cull was annoyed by it as well, he told me so one day in the palace gardens.

I miss it there. The technomancers do a fine job of horticulture or, landscape architecture. Not sure what you'd call it. They made floating platforms which move around so that the scenery always changes. Although it must be said that there would be changes if I were the type to complain. Some buffoon managed to install follies among all the trees and flowers and waterfalls and whatnot. Have you seen? Columns, ruined arches, that kind of thing. Perverse.

I was actually sitting on one of those awful ruins on the day I spoke to Cull in there. I was painting. A couple of techs had gone up with me to make sure that I could get back down, which put me slightly on edge. The technomancers are uncanny. I really hate their faces. I feel sorry for them, obviously. Seems like such a horrific punishment for being so skilled.

I know Military all have enhancements too. And Red faction ambassadors have to get their real hands removed for the prosthetics which looks painful, but you can forget about it in a way you can't forget about a technomancer's jaw. It looks so inhumane, it's like you should be able to hear the hard metal grinding against the flesh of their faces while they talk. You can see the gears ticking as they think. Horrible. Also, I fucked one of them when I was blackout drunk one night in the capital but I have no idea which, so I have no choice but to treat them all like people I have been physically inside. Very inconvenient.

Anyway. I had my books of poetry with me, a novel I was working on, and my paints. I must have looked like a complete and utter fool. Who does that? The empire was falling into pieces. We were being attacked by some evil god thing and I was composing landscapes in the garden. There was one particularly beautiful oak which I had requested be positioned in front of the rockery for the occasion. Stunning. I bet they were all laughing at me.

Cull's appearance took me by surprise. I hadn't heard him coming but there he was, suddenly by my side and completely alone. He had no business being that stealthy.

"Beautiful," he told me, scaring me half to death and making me shriek like a baby. He smiled—a little, unapologetic twitch of the lips. "I always wished I was left-handed."

It struck me that this was the strangest thing you could possibly say to a person who has just shrieked at you. It's strange anyway, who would ever want to be left-handed? What use is it? What use is being right-handed? What did he mean? I wish I'd asked. But under the circumstances it seemed downright unkind, like he was mocking me.

Perhaps he was mocking me, perhaps what he meant was that the only desirable thing about me was left-handedness, which isn't desirable at all.

Am I thinking too much into it? I know you don't care. You told me to think aloud and that's what I'm doing. Yes, I know I'm pathetic. May I pour you some more wine?

"Oh, sorry," I said, but I don't know what I was sorry for. Existing, maybe.

"May I sit?" Cull asked, indicating the marble to my right. I nodded, and he did. I felt trapped, apprehended. I just carried on painting as if he wasn't there.

It was a long time before he spoke again. "Rhododendron told me that you would probably be up here."

"Oh," I said, "my brother sent you to find me?"

"No." He raised his hands, which I can remember because he had a little notepad. His left thumb, curled over the top page, was covered in black marks. He roughed his pen over its knuckle and added even more of them before he made a note in a script that I could not understand. "I asked him where you were."

"Oh." It occurred to me then that I was saying "oh" a lot, and that I should probably take some initiative. "Why do you do that?"

"What?"

"With your pen. Why have you scribbled all over your thumb?"

He smiled in the way he had when I had shrieked at him and held up the thumb for our mutual inspection as he replied, "I like to write with a ballpoint. It never works when you first put it to paper, you have to get the ball rolling."

"Is that a metaphor?" I asked, like a fucking idiot.

"No." He lowered the thumb.

I carried on painting. Ruining the canvas. It had been a stunning study in block colors, but with him watching me I was just wrecking it.

"You appear to be ruining that canvas."

"Yes, well," I said, annoyed as well as embarrassed, "I'm not used to being observed." As if I was some mysterious operatic composer rather than a hobbyist on a rock.

"Shall I leave?"

"Oh. You, don't have to," I said. Or something.

"Stop for a while then, I feel terrible that I'm ruining your . . . what shall we call it? Artistic air up here."

I smiled and hoped he thought I was in on whatever joke it sounded like he was trying to make. "Certainly. Can I help you?"

He shrugged. "Well. No. And perhaps yes. I want your acquaintance, and you can give it to me."

I definitely blushed. He must have seen so and decided to spare me the humiliation because he stood up and walked to the edge of the grassy platform, hands behind his back. I followed when I felt I had my face in order.

"Do you and Rhododendron have opposite hairstyles on purpose?" I saw then that Rhododendron was what he was looking at. The Red emperor surrounded by his friends, water trickling past them as they laughed.

I told Cull that we had always had "opposite hairstyles" when we were children because our mother thought that it was absurd for twins to dress the same, especially ones who look so unalike. There was more to it than that of course, but I was trying to be charming. You're not supposed to know who our biological parents are, and with Rhododendron's hair it was just too obvious that at least one of them was from the Caralla family; that's why he kept himself clean-shaven. I can't guess who my parents were. I'm not interested, the Red emperor was my real mother as far as I'm concerned. Yes, it is true. You're not interested in your mother either, Ming. You haven't asked me about Adora at all even though you know she must still be in the palace somewhere. I'm sorry, forgive me, I'm getting tipsy.

Cull and I sat on the edge of the platform together for some time, being uncouth about Daksha and Vard's romance. He kept alluding to the fact that he would like Red and Green to be closer, too. Was that flirting? Did he mean he wanted to fuck me? Or Rhododendron? Perverse. I don't think Rhododendron ever had any sexual partners anyway. He was always surrounded by black hands and surely you can't sleep with them because the actual hands are so horrible.

May I ask a question? Are you sad that you never got your prosthetic hands? You must have been moments away from your amputation. You did all that work climbing the ranks just to do this whole overthrowing thing right when you were about to be promoted. No? Fascinating. Anyway, pardon me.

After that, Cull asked me if he could ask a personal question. I said of course, which I should not have, and so he said, "Do you like being in the Red faction?"

I could not believe that I had been asked such a thing. What kind of question is that for a person?

"It's just that, the rest of us all choose. I chose to be Green, Daksha chose to be an Ethicist. Vard is the most Military person you could imagine. As far as I can see, you and Rhododendron are the only two people in the entire empire who didn't get a choice. What happens if a child is born to the Red succession who doesn't want to be emperor?"

This was stunning to me. Utterly true, but completely shocking. It was like being asked why you were born, but sincerely, and in a way which suddenly makes you hate your mother.

"The person in charge should be under the most scrutiny." is what I said. No idea why.

Cull used his eyebrows to agree with me that this was in fact a non sequitur, so I tried again.

"It is so important to the system that I have no choice in the matter that I have never thought about the fact of it."

He smiled then, in a way which showed me I had chosen the right option.

"Are you looking forward to Hecubah?" he asked, after a long and comfortable pause.

"No," I scoffed, "it's going to be a nightmare." He asked why, and I should not have told him the truth but I was thrilled by his proximity and so I did. "Avon Stal is a difficult person. Her ship . . . it's not just a warship. I know Vard said so but it isn't. It's practically a palace just like the Zetland. It's huge, self-sustaining, population of thousands. Never lands. And it's safe right now. She may not want to risk it."

Cull frowned. "You don't think she will help when she knows the full extent of what's happening back home?"

I shrugged.

"Why?"

I told him the truth again, I told him that I wouldn't if it were me.

After that day I thought of Cull constantly. For no reason. I didn't know him, so it was pure narcissism. I fancied myself getting close to the Green emperor, getting out of Rhododendron's shadow and forming that special allegiance which Daksha and Vard flaunted over the rest of us. All the hours I spent painting or writing I would fantasize that he would see it, imagined what he'd say and how I would respond. How impressed he would be, the gossip everyone would spread about us. I even started wearing corsets just in case he came to speak with me again. I got the idea into my head that he liked femininity, you see. I don't know how I could bear the obsession, how much it made me hate myself.

Other people noticed, too. There was one particular morning, I was standing in front of my mirror, watching myself getting laced into one of those monstrous corsets, when I caught Clara's eye in the glass. She was still in bed, covers pulled over her shoulders and her feet kicking over the edge of the mattress. I could tell she was thinking something unpleasant.

"What?" I said, when the eye contact made her smile.

"I'm laughing at you," she answered.

"I can see that," I replied, trying to maintain a pleasant tone, "any chance I'll find out why?"

The deodand behind me patted my back to show that he was finished tying the lace, so I went back over to find Clara within the deluge of cushions that she demanded of me. She giggled and then gasped when I caught her, probably from the cold on my hands. I didn't let go. I didn't like it when she laughed at me and so I was being rough with her. I pinned her beneath me, trying to make her tell me what was funny. She liked it, so she was refusing. I fucked her and felt no better for it.

Rhododendron noticed too, of course. He told me I looked like a prick.

"You look like a prick, Speaker."

I just said good morning and sat down.

We were in the Red office. When the Zetland is stationary the walls are transparent so that each faction can see when another is holding a meeting. The entire capital can see, in fact, but we were in space where it's closed with metal shutters so spacefreaks can't distract us. We used to have meetings up there sometimes which were nothing more than us standing around looking busy, images of us broadcast to the newscreens throughout the capital to assure people that whatever their problems are we're "on it." I always wondered if the other factions did that too. I suppose I shall never know, now, with everyone being mostly dead and all. But that morning was a serious meeting, we were finally nearing Hecubah, and we had word from Avon Stal. That must be the biggest benefit of being Red, we almost always get messages first.

The message was in the centre of the table, a big digital screen lit with LED. Tiny little lights forming the message in real time. Sounds like it should be easy, doesn't it? But the technomancers watched it like it was a wild animal. It always reminded me of a deep-sea creature. Flashing, throbbing, flowing red dots. What am I saying, you're a Ming, I'm sure you understand it better than I do. I can't quite remember what the glyph Avon sent said. Something like, hello, descend, welcome, safe. She may have added a radical here or there that meant that it was a shitshow.

Rhododendron was worried regardless. He was at his most beautiful when he was anxious, all the shards of metal under his skin would glow slightly as he used them. We'd done that on purpose, making his modifications visible so that he appeared honest, so that anybody speaking to him could see which parts of his bioware he was actively using. Mother's idea. Completely unnecessary of course, Rhododendron would never lie.

He looked at his glowing wrist and said, "There are five thousand six hundred and eighty-four people in the palace."

I wish I hadn't but I said, "So?"

He sighed, and Adora Ming shot me one of her looks before ignoring me and putting her prosthetic black hand on his shoulder, "They'll be alright."

"Platitudes," he said, and the back of his wrists glowed to show that he was making a note. "I think that we should leave them in safety. They aren't soldiers, many aren't even factioned. There are children. We could leave the Zetland on Hecubah and board Avon's warship instead."

That was just like him. I had thought he was as worried about Avon Stal's loyalty as I, but he was just too good. Thinking about the people instead.

There were of course a million reasons we could not commandeer Avon's warship. Adora listed about a dozen of them before he conceded.

When we conveyed Avon's message to the other emperors it cheered them up in a way it hadn't Rhododendron. Their enthusiasm softened him a little.

"Knew she'd have things in order down there," said Vard, with a grin.

Daksha told him not to gloat. She called him sweetheart.

"I am not gloating," he replied, smiling not just to Daksha but to the Ethicists behind her, "I am expressing pleasure at . . ."

"Being right?" supplied Cull, sitting now on a throne, still with his notepad and his inky thumb.

They all laughed, everyone except for Ella—the Military steward. I absolutely hated him at the time so I could never stop myself from looking at him. Older than we are but appearing twenty-five with all the cosmetics and always swaggering around in a vexing manner.

I had the most bizarre and unpleasant exchange with him one time in the bar up in the Ethicists' quadrant. Beautiful place, one of the most easy-going of all the social spaces outside of the Red dives. Like any Ethicist or Green bar you've ever been in, with the sharks and the pianos and all that, but it was always dark and laid out in such a way that it was possible to politely pretend you hadn't noticed the people sitting nearby. Perfect space for the most famous of us to be around in semipublic without being spoken to.

That is not to say that the Red faction dive bars aren't fun, but they all play that industrial techno music that it's impossible to dance to over the age of twenty without looking like you were bullied as a child.

Anyway, the bar was full of blue Military uniforms that night. Ella was one of them, screeching and showing off. I had Clara and a couple of the others at my table but only for the sake of background noise and someone to talk to the waiters for me if I wanted anything. I was not in a conversational mood and I had a new translation of Hegel to get through.

"Fifty-fifty vodka martini with three blue cheese olives," trilled the waiter as he came over to our table and placed the drink in front of me. "I knew you had to be around here somewhere when I saw the bartender putting it together."

I looked up then, but I should have known it was him to begin with. Why would a waiter announce what I was drinking?

"Oh, hello Ella," I said, and tried to make him Clara's problem by kicking her under the table. "Thank you."

"So I asked him if he wouldn't mind if I brought it over to you. Wine, darlings? I've got some fruit and bread for you too." Ella poured their wine for them with a theatrical servitude which made them all giggle. I tried to pretend I wasn't there. "Speaker doesn't feed you I suppose, you poor beautiful creatures. Have you ever seen Speaker eat something that isn't drenched in vodka? That's why you're so skinny, darling."

I tried to appear game as he slid into the booth beside Clara, although the comment had ruined my olive. I wasn't skinny, I was svelte. Clara seized on this line of conversation as a good way to distract the brute and started giving him faux-juicy titbits about me that of course everybody already knew.

"Not just any vodka," she said, winking at him, "only the one with the silver top will do."

"My my what a little fusspot," he replied and then put his actual arm around her shoulders. To her credit, one of the other girls managed to mitigate the arm by taking his hand and making an ordeal over how beautiful his rings were, which he then distributed for them all to wear. Bastard. I mean, at the time. Bastard at the time.

"So, Speaker," he began, just as I had decided he was only interested in Clara and returned to my book, "how do you feel about Avon Stal?"

I placed the book on the table and dismissed my entourage with a nod. When we were alone I said, "What do you want to know and why?"

He laughed. I ignored him and ate an olive. "Darling, why do you have to be so serious? I'm just making conversation now that we're all on this little adventure together."

"Adventure?"

"To find Avon Stal," he said, in the same tone you would use to remind someone that knives are sharp and that you happen to be holding one.

I shrugged. "Oh."

"You think you're better than me?" he asked, completely out of nowhere.

"I don't think anything."

His eyes flashed to the book on the table and I picked it up again, protective almost. Embarrassed. "Looks like you do. Looks like you think a lot." he said, "Or is that all a show?"

"I have no idea what you're talking about."

He laughed again. "I'm sorry, yes. You're right. I'm interrupting."

Weird, right? Maybe he was dunk or something.

Anyway he stood up as if to leave and placed his hand flat on the table right in front of me before he did. "Tell your friends they can give me my rings back in person, whenever they feel like it."

Then he was gone before I could tell him to go fuck himself. Not that I would have anyway. I got drunk enough that night that I fell asleep on the couch in my suite. Ella's rings were in my pocket when I woke up, but I don't know how they got there.

4

We didn't make a ceremony of leaving the Zetland. Would have been embarrassing. Everybody knew we were going down to Hecubah to beg help from someone with enough power to say no. I think that's the real reason Vard didn't go with us. There was a chance Avon Stal would refuse, and if she had done so to him then his authority as Military emperor would have been compromised.

Clara was with us, thank goodness, but I was annoyed with her. I hadn't wanted her to come, probably because I still thought I might be able to seduce Cull. But I couldn't tell Clara that, and none of my protestations that there were necromancers and witches and all sorts of other villainy I made up down there had worked. Nobody on the descending vessel liked that she was there either, she wasn't even a faction member. I think she enjoyed their disdain. Adora Ming also didn't accompany us, which was unusual. She's the unofficial leader of the Red diplomats, as you know, but the Mings were laying low because of, ah, well because of you. We all knew that there was a Ming on Apech when the invasion began. We didn't know that it was you leading Apech against us, of course, we just thought you'd failed to prevent the attack.

Anyway, we thought we were fucked when we set eyes on the place. It was malaria nirvana down there. We had all our vaccines before descending but there was a collective horror noise in the landing ship when we broke into visibility. It's a swamp. This is what happens when you don't have a strong centralised state, you know. Swamps. Lizards galore. But I already felt triple fucked because I had both Avon Stal and Clara to contend with on top of the mosquitoes.

Surely you've met Avon before, Ming? Yes, I thought you would have. The de-aging on her is absurd. She must be nearing ninety but looks, what would you say, seventeen? And not in a pretty way. Not that I think seventeen-year-olds are pretty. Well, some of them are. But not like that. I mean she looks youthful in an affected, dollish way. A mockery of beauty, like she's flaunting over you that she's wearing a skinsuit, that you'll never see her for what she really is. She's terrifying, basically. Perhaps it's because of the way she moves or her expressions, but everything about her screams that the soul in the body is nothing like the face. Or maybe it's just that you know she's a brutal wardog who has chosen to look like a child's toy. She's made herself into an ostentatiously venomous thing.

She was there when we landed, snaking over to meet us with the rest of the Stals and a few Pïat-Elementovs. I did rather admire what she had done with her uniform, though—a Military blue dress with a spectacularly long skirt and clever sleeves. A few strands of silk which ran from her shoulders to the rings around her middle fingers. So you could see all of her battle scars, though her wounds could be artificial too for all I know. Probably are.

The deodands threw themselves to the ground when we approached her, which was particularly embarrassing because, as I say, it was a swamp. More a squelch than a bow. I don't know what I was thinking wearing suede.

"Speaker," she said, and I was flattered that she came to me first. Even her voice was creepy. It was validating if disappointing to learn from Cull's reaction to her that he definitely was attracted that kind of look. Knew it. "And Your New Majesty." She fluttered her evil eyelashes at him all cutely. "Welcome to Hecubah."

"General." Cull took her hand and kissed it—I've never seen anything so bourgeois. "What a pleasure to meet you."

She giggled. I wanted to die. She's been tried for war crimes on three separate occasions. It's ridiculous, nobody else gets to do war crimes.

Her entourage led us through a dirt path in the swamp to a large canvas tent ahead. It smelled rather promisingly of fire and booze.

I walked a pace behind Avon and Cull the whole way, trying to feign slight disinterest, but self-consciousness got the better of me so I interrupted to say, "I imagine the swampland makes foundations impossible, for solid building?"

"Not quite." She raised her hand to indicate the locals who were following us at our periphery, their eyes fixed on our heavily armed deodands. "See the guards?"

Cull looked with me. He said, "I confess, I did not realize they were guards."

She giggled again, suggesting that he was onto something. Jealous, I said the obvious as if I had spotted it first. "They're unarmed."

"Exactly," she said, and her voice for once sounded real. There was joy in it, a growling excitement shuddering up through her usual childishness. Perverse. "They don't need to be. Those are pyromancers and conjurers."

"Are we in danger?" asked Cull. No, that was me. "Are we in danger?"

She laughed. "Of course. But the tents help. They cannot always control what they summon, better to be under collapsing fabric than concrete, no?"

Then she told us that she knew we hadn't been properly briefed on the planet since she took up residence there, that she was about to introduce us to the leaders of the three most powerful schools of magic, which were conjuration, psychokinesis, and godsforsaken necromancy. You wouldn't think necromancy would be of much use, considering they can't control the people they revive. The necromanced become flesh ghosts, zombies doing whatever it was they were doing last—which is why the necromancers were so important. Hecubah's dead served as bodyguards, builders, musicians, dancers. Relentlessly performing the action they died doing. It's a form of punishment, you know. Those with power over minds would instill desire in them, say to keep wineglasses full, another would deal the death blow, and then the necromancer would have them breathing into dead lungs before their heart missed a beat. Puppets until the necromancer dies. Also perverse.

"The psychokinetics are the ones with the hats." Her tone showed that "the hats" was nothing good. "More like helmets. They wear them at public events like this as a courtesy, to show they aren't influencing our decisions."

"Do they work?" asked Cull, who still hadn't recovered from whatever her foul visage was doing to his body.

Avon stopped then, just in front of the tent. "Your Highnesses," she teased, consciously reminding us I suspect that we outranked her in name only, "I have no idea."

She should not have done that. It meant that both Cull and I emerged into the tent with expressions of bewildered alarm rather than, I don't know, stateliness.

Nothing of note happened on that first meeting, not until we were alone with Avon. The feast was spectacular, the tent lovely. It was all informal, sitting on rugs and furs on the ground to eat. The space was heated by the conjurers, who had created animals of harmless, glowing fire which would walk around between us, nuzzling and sleeping as if real. I have a drawing of one here if you—okay never mind. Wolves, boars, that kind of thing. We exchanged all our gifts and pleasantries. I really did start to feel optimistic. None of Avon's people seemed to think that Apech or the Apechi god were going to be a problem at all.

Another thing I did notice was that the three leaders were the only ones wearing translators, which I found slightly ominous because Avon must have had hundreds at her disposal. Why deny them communication? But Clara was charming her way through everyone without the need for language. They were delighted by her, showing off for her with parlour tricks and other such nonsense. I was wearing a brand-new jacket but nobody mentioned it.

The only hiccup was the head necromancer. I took an immediate dislike to him and found myself unable to remain entirely polite. It wasn't necessarily the nature of his craft that put me off so much, though of course that didn't help. It was his shoes. They had skulls on them. Embroidered skulls. Dickhead.

We weren't shown to where we were staying until well after midnight, which is when the conversation took a serious turn. It shouldn't have done, we were all far too tipsy, but there was so much that Avon wanted to know. It was almost an interrogation. She probably planned the whole thing to turn out like that.

Our tent was as large as the one we ate in, but with low wooden beams where they'd hung additional furs to separate into different bedrooms. Cull and I were shown to the largest, where a fire-bear lay sleeping between two fur beds. I know it's decadent but we should get some furs in here, they're really delightful. Clara sulked because she'd been sent to another bedroom and sulked even more when Avon came into ours with us. I found that bit of jealousy very cute of her, imagine thinking Avon Stal would want to fuck me. Cull poured more wine in his excitement about Avon's presence, I should have stopped him.

"Do forgive us making you bunk up like this." She flopped herself onto what I then assumed was Cull's bed, "It was my idea, thought you'd prefer having a space to talk." She was speaking at a high, clear volume, not at all like we were in a tent. I assumed that it was soundproofed somehow.

"Is it soundproofed somehow, in here?" I asked.

She laughed. "Of course."

Cull handed me a glass first, then her. We toasted to Crysth, which I realize is uninspired but felt necessary in the circumstances.

"Tell me, then. Tell me how bad it is."

I answered for us both. I told her that our ambassador on Apech had been killed. The Military ship, which had arrived to investigate, had been disabled by a deity residing on Apech that had the ability to infect and then manipulate sentient beings—even the very low-grade sentience of the demons that power most of the empire's machines. We were infected, immobile. I told her that it was a relatively bloodless battle even when they came to the capital; their deity blew up Juniper and then simply turned everything off.

Once I had finished explaining, she said, "So the government has fallen."

Cull choked on his wine, and I didn't know what to say either so I said, "No, no. We still have the emperors and the Zetland."

She smiled and rearranged her skirt, distracting us both with a view of her horribly scarred thighs. "You can watch but not control, flee but not attack. They have taken the capital. Vard is emperor only of the Zetland," she turned to Cull, "and so are you."

He just stared at her. It was the first time I'd seen him do something unattractive.

"So what we need to do . . ." She stood up and her tone changed completely. She began to pace, walking back and forth through the sleeping bear. I didn't like that, it seemed rude. I know the bear wasn't real but it was so tranquil and she was ruining it. "We need an exorcism."

Cull snapped back to himself at that word, "Yes! Exactly. Can we do that?"

"The deity appears to be Apech's only strength. They obviously cannot meet us in combat. We will be dealing with . . . repercussions of it for decades, but the first thing we can do is get their magic out of our ships."

"How?" I asked.

"I have an idea. I need to speak to Vard about it first, but I have an idea."

Cull and I shared a glance, excited and scared. She wasn't supposed to have been able to pull her ship off the grid, give her techs the ability to think and move without being monitored by central—but she had. And so perhaps she could do more.

"But it won't work," she mused to herself, putting down her glass and beginning to think with her hands.

"Why?" asked Cull.

She shook her head for a long time before responding. "We don't know how this deity, virus, whatever it is actually spreads. It will infect us. We need to freeze it, stop its ability to move. Only then can we start to push it back. Where are our deimancers? Why could they not control it?"

"The entire ring of experts was killed. Apech assassinated them along with Juniper," he said with such an incredible sadness. I don't know why I didn't pay more attention to that sound. There was something there.

"How can that be possible? They are our best." It sounded like an accusation, and she was right to be suspicious. I still don't know the answer. They were just no resistance to it, the god of Apech flattened our deimancers like they were nothing.

"Our best weren't good enough." I think I was the one who said that.

"No," she agreed, "no. That's our problem." She stopped her pacing. "We teach everyone in the empire that deities are to be feared, hated, destroyed. We do it with language even when we're not saying it outright. We use this obscure phraseology which stops people from actually *thinking* about what we're looking at. Demons. Gods. Even calling the techs 'technomancers,' have you ever thought about that? 'Deimancer'? Ridiculous. It's a process of rendering meaningless. Making people stupid." Her voice was breaking into that growl again, the real her surfacing under the synthetics. Fascinating, really. "So those with the skill to communicate with *deities*," and I could hear disdain for the word, "even to control them, do so without tact or understanding. Just brute force. They are rigid and so they snap. What we need is a believer."

We waited for more, but all she said was that she needed to discuss matters with Vard.

We were excited when she was gone. It felt like a plan again. We had another drink, even, sitting on the furs at the head of the bear.

5

Ming drummed her fingers on the bathroom tile. "You are sad," she said.

Speaker had been engrossed in their reading, making little notes as they went along. They had not noticed the monster as she moved.

She was on the edge of the tub, her brutalized torso exposed to the hip. Her eyes were wide, fixed on the tears dripping down Speaker's face. Speaker stared back, motionless in the focus of her attention.

"Why?" she asked, bringing a foot up over the side of the tub to sit on its side. Water oozed from her scars.

Speaker raised their hands to indicate the bathroom, the world at large. "Everything."

"No." She stood upright and took her empty glass in hand. "Something about the story, now, is making you cry. What is it?"

"Cull?" suggested Speaker, the rising tone at the end of the word containing not just a question but a plea.

"Think about it."

Speaker watched her retreating back, panic rising in their chest. "I . . ."

"You."

Speaker heard the cork leave the wine bottle, followed by liquid. "We thought that we had solved it."

"Solved it." She turned around, stalking back to Speaker with the bottle in her hand.

"Yes. I mean, we thought that we had made the right decision, everything was going so well. Avon had a plan, she and Vard were going to carry it out. We felt . . . I felt like I had done something. The wine was good, the room was comfortable. The bear was warm. It was perfect. It was, the last time I was happy."

Ming sat beside Speaker. Speaker did not look at her face, did not dare. They could feel her breath on their ear, smell her bleeding mouth. Hated themself for having noticed her hard nipples, the perfumed water dripping over them.

"Self-pity." Her voice.

More tears from Speaker's eyes, unquenchable fear. "No. Nostalgia. Regret."

"Nostalgia"—she filled Speaker's glass—"is self-pity. What do you regret?"

"Cull." Speaker.

"That you never fucked him?"

"No!" too soon, too defensive. "No."

"Then what?" Ming.

"That I couldn't save him. That I didn't even know he needed saving."

She relaxed, crossed her legs. "Maybe he didn't. Maybe one of those mind-control people got to him."

"No. It was there inside him, whatever it was. I could see it once it happened, retrospectively." Their chin wobbled, their voice broke. Ming studied the way their shoulders shuddered as they sobbed.

She drained her glass, began to breathe deeply.

Speaker watched her. Shallow breaths shook water from her face, eyes screwed shut, hands clenching and unclenching.

Speaker almost felt concern. "Ming," they asked, "what are you doing?"

She opened her eyes to look back at her prisoner. Bloodshot.

"Are you . . . Gods, are you trying to cry?"

She grimaced and stood, waving the tips of her fingers in the air in a gesture which looked designed to dismiss thought.

"Crying is not the key to this." Speaker.

"What do you think the key is, then? Why does it want you? What could it possibly be," she spat, "that my god likes so much about you?"

"Likes?" Speaker gaped in disbelief. "If this infection is fondness then what could be hate? Bone grew out of my skin! How could you think that it *likes* me?"

Ming blinked, caught off guard. "Wrong verb," she said, after a while. "It finds you useful, desirable."

But not you, thought Speaker, and they realized that they were gloating.

Speaker is infected, sacrosanct. The god of Apech has forced itself into their body much in the same way it forced itself into the Crysthian fleet. Ming has been trying to coax the Apechi godvirus into her ever since she found it, but it will not listen to her. All she can do is study Speaker, try to find whatever quality they have that led her god into them, then try to make it a part of herself.

Speaker shook their head. "You know I don't know why."

"But you have your suspicions."

"No, I don't. It's just . . . everyone cries. Everyone would be sad, under the circumstances. So that can't be it, otherwise the god would have infected everyone. It's just me, right?"

Ming sighed, defeated. Briefly human.

"Yes. It's just you. Tell me about it, then. The last time you were happy."

6

There's nothing much more to say. I was sitting so close to Cull that I could see his flaws, little lines around his eyes and forehead, a scar on his lower lip. He was stunning. Not conventionally attractive, just beautiful. Light, airy. Always looking like he was about to laugh, supremely confident in a boyish, cooperative way. I wish I had painted him. It's so difficult to compose a portrait from memory, although I suppose it's more honest that way. Painting what someone is rather than what they look like.

But it didn't last long, the moment of peace, because that's when I spotted the rock. It was in the basket we had been gifted by the conjurers, full of mostly little colorful balls that would turn into something pretty when you threw them up in the air. That's why it caught my eye, just a rock. I swear it hadn't been there before.

"What's that?" He turned to drag the basket toward us.

"Something innocuous I hope," he said.

I remember that because, unfortunately, I did actually say "irockuous," which he had the grace to ignore.

He rolled it over in his hands before passing it to me with his lip sticking out in a cute, puzzled way. I was holding it down to the light of the bear's face when he said, "Oh no."

I almost dropped it, glad I didn't. I half thought he'd spotted a pin and it was actually a grenade, but the "oh no" seemed a little too calm for that.

He took it back from me, inserted his thumbnails into a crack on the side. I told him to wait but he had already started exerting force.

"Oh no," he said again, when two halves of rock cradled one piece of paper between them. "Not secret messages." He read it. "Oh no! Not 'meet behind the feast tent before dawn.'"

I shared his sentiment. Everything had seemed to be going so well. What I said was, "Gods, we're not doing sedition etcetera are we?"

"When even is 'before dawn'? Now?"

I shrugged and checked Zetland time, which was useless, then covered the action by saying, "Who do you think it is?"

"Well it isn't Avon. She doesn't strike me as a putter of secret messages in rocks. Plus the handwriting is awful, non-native. Who the hell is putting secret messages in rocks?"

"Witch people."

"Oh no. You're probably right. This has witch people all over it. We need to get rid of it."

"Pretend we haven't seen it?"

"I don't know yet. Let's just get rid of it. It's evidence."

"Burn it."

"With what? Shall I just rip it up?"

"Eat it." I can't believe I told him to eat it. Anyway I ended up eating it.

He brought me some wine to wash it down with, still laughing.

"Now what?" I asked him, and he shrugged. "We're not going, are we?"

He took a long drink and then looked at me with all that boyishness he had about his old face. "I kinda want to."

"No! We need to tell Avon."

He seemed to like the idea of getting her back but was still reluctant, saying, "What if it's *about* her?"

"Even more reason to tell her." I was right. "We do not want to get involved with anything she wouldn't like. Seriously. She is a frightening person. We should be scared."

"Oh come on." He winked at me, which was unfair. "It's not every day an emperor of Crysth gets to go sneaking around a swamp. There's nothing here, no spies no roads no . . . You know, nothing. This might be the last bit of fun I ever have. Let's not ruin it by making it official."

"But it's dark! Do you think we can take the bear?" I tried making some encouraging noises at aforesaid, but it was unmoved by my effort.

He told me he had a torch in his forearm, which I should have asked more about because why would someone who isn't a soldier have a forearm torch? I had one in my cheek for reading once, but the shadow of my nose got on my nerves too much. He walked like Military when we were out there, too. Forearm horizontal in front of his chest, pistol resting on top of it. I reminded him that Avon had told us there was no point being armed, but he told me to bring my seeking knife anyway. "You never know," he said. "It'll be fun."

The deodands were easy to get past. Alarmingly so, in fact. They must have realized the futility of their armaments because they weren't even trying. I snitched on them to Rhododendron when we got back. He told me to get over it.

The journey was uneventful saving for us both needing to pee, which was completely undignified. For me, anyway. Cull seemed delighted by the whole thing. He was elected as steward right at the start of Juniper's term of office, so it must have been decades since he got to do anything without an army around him. Me too, but I don't care. My inner world is satisfying enough.

Anyway you know the punch line already. It was the fucking necromancer waiting for us. He was still wearing those embroidered skull shoes—no idea how they weren't filthy, my boots were ruined. Probably witchery. He was there to conspire, which is humiliating. His name was "Zhim" which I'm spelling "Z-h-i-m" because "Jim" with a "J" is too good for him.

After we'd recovered from the initial shock of there actually being someone to meet us, he said, "I wasn't expecting you to come alone, Your Highnesses." Hecuban is quite a lovely language, sort of like chanting. It jarred with the translator he was wearing, which spoke in a low baritone nothing at all like the hymns coming from his mouth.

Cull laughed at that. "You know, I just assumed we were supposed to. Let's call it starting on trust."

He led us a five-minute or so walk away to another tent, which in retrospect we really, really shouldn't have gone to. Could have been anything waiting for us, but honestly a trap may have been more entertaining than a tent full of necromancers and dead servants. And they served us tea. Who wants tea "before dawn"? It was all so vulgar.

By that point Cull was having an excellent time, though. I was not. I had sobered up a little on the walk and realized how stupid we were being, but I was propelled by a desire to look confident and useful in front of him.

He was so polite all the time. We sat around the little table drinking the godsawful tea and there was this teenager, or, you know, what we thought was a teenager, trying to take off his jacket. Cull said, "May I enquire as to what this young man is doing?"

One of the necromancers said something to Zhim, oh you know what it's unbearable I'm going to spell it with a J. One of the necromancers said something to Jim and he translated, "Your Highness, please forgive us but his master says that he will become violent if you do not allow him to remove the jacket. He just wants to clean it."

I saw Cull wince and quickly suppress it as he realized. "He's dead?"

Jim nodded.

My jacket was much nicer than Cull's, and it was new. Why it went for his rather than mine I have no idea. I never get anything.

I started looking around then to see if I could tell who was dead and who was alive, which turned out to be comfortingly easy. The dead stare. They are utterly fixated on their task, glaring at whatever it is they're possessed to do. One of the not-Jim necromancers saw me looking and demonstrated the advantage of their own corpse servant by crumbling bread onto the floor, which distressed the dead man so much that he whined like a dog the whole time he spent cleaning it up. Perverse.

The mood was pretty relaxed for a tent full of conspirators and death. I'm sure it's the Hecuban interior design, all the furs and rugs. There were no fire animals there, though, just plain lamps. I suppose the necromancers can't sustain them without conjurers. Plus, Cull was being incredibly easy, chatting away like it was lunchtime on a riverboat cruise regardless of the fact that most of the people he was talking to couldn't understand a word he was saying or were, you know, actually fucking dead.

"So," he started, putting his hands flat on the low table between us and suddenly appearing formal. "Why did you put a slip of paper in a rock?"

Jim smiled apologetically and said, "The majority cannot know that you are here."

His people clearly did not like that they could not understand Cull's responses, they kept demanding translations which we could tell were accurate because Jim couldn't turn off the translator. It made the conversation a bit of a nightmare, stilted and repetitive, but we got there in the end. I'm paraphrasing obviously.

What he said was, "The majority do not want your general to leave. The presence of your empire heralded an unprecedented time of peace and cooperation among our people. Your help in defeating the god of magnetism and its monks was invaluable. We didn't know you could do that. We have come so far with your help, and many fear that the absence of your general in times of war for your empire would signal the end of our relationship."

Cull managed to be incredibly serious, not putting a single diplomatic hair out of place. It was impressive.

"Sir," he said, "we are delighted to hear that Crysth's diplomatic mission has been carried out with such success on your planet. I understand that many of your fellows have already joined general Avon Stal's ranks on a temporary basis, and under normal circumstances we would have a black hand ambassador of the Red faction"—he indicated me and my maroon outfit then, so I nodded in a serious way—"stationed on your planet already. Along, of course, with Hecuban representation on the capital planet itself.

Apech's invasion, unfortunately, renders this impossible. Crysth needs Avon's expertise in order to dispel their assault."

There was a whole debacle while he translated this back to everyone else. Then there was an argument about what to say next. Then Jim said, "We know. The others plan to keep her here by force if necessary."

At that, Cull's expression dropped into this incredible rage. I couldn't believe his face could perform such a feat. He looked so angry. It was just for a second, but it was enough. Contempt.

Jim put his hands in the air and said, "I am not threatening you or her. I would never. We think this is a disastrous idea. We"—he flapped his arms around to indicate that "we" was the tent—"want to come with you. We want to help. We want to solidify the diplomatic ties between Crysth and Hecubah, to ensure that we will be members of the empire once Apech has been defeated. We have experience fighting with what you call deities now! We can help. Ultimately, we are very concerned that the others may not let her ship leave us unless we have this connection. And we want to make sure it's us, those of us who would not consider harming a member of the empire, who represent Hecubah." It was then that I realized that the Hecuban word for "Hecubah" was not "Hecubah." Pretty tasteless of whoever called it Hecubah if you ask me. "We fear that the more . . . rash among us, may do something to sabotage our future."

Cull looked at me then. I just nodded, because it seemed like a good idea to me, but he obviously disagreed. "Why have you not brought this up with Avon Stal directly?"

Jim seemed on the verge of laughter. When he translated to the others some of them did laugh, which I could tell really annoyed Cull. Annoyed him so much he couldn't hide it, in fact.

"Care to let me in on the joke?" is what he said.

"Pardon us. It's just that, your general Avon Stal has been living with us for a long time now—a relationship which began with her attacking us. We have come to know her. What you are seeing here is, you must understand, a desperate attempt. Message in a rock is not a good idea, we know this. We come to you, the other Crysth factions, because we are afraid what would happen to our people if she knew some of us planned to hold her hostage."

Cull raised his eyebrows, said, "Ah."

He looked at me again, so I said, "I am in agreement that taking any form of hostile action whatsoever against Avon Stal would be inadvisable." Can you imagine. She would crack that planet like an egg.

"Yes, we agree." Jim said, nodding fit to break his own neck.

I couldn't tell what Cull was thinking but he said, "So what you want is for us to negotiate the presence of a Hecuban emissary aboard our ships without divulging the information that not doing so would be tantamount to war between our people?"

I wish he hadn't phrased it like that. It put everyone on edge. We left soon after, with very little resolved. But it just didn't seem like a big deal to me. Of course they wanted to be a part of Crysth and of course Avon Stal is terrifying. Coming to us was a good idea, even if they executed it poorly. It bothered Cull though, I don't know why. He couldn't not know how fantastic the optics would be of us having a very new addition to the empire on our side in the war against Apech.

"Do you Reds have to put up with this kind of thing all the time, or is it just me?" he asked me when we were back in the room.

"You wanted to go," is what I said, petulant and defensive. I didn't like "you Reds" for some reason, and I was annoyed by how annoyed he was. It made no sense to me. It was just a bit of a caper, some provincials making a fuss about something that we could resolve with a wave of a hand.

"Yes." He sighed at me. "It was nice seeing the look on the deodands' faces when we came back though, wasn't it?" I watched him for a while before he spoke again. He had his eyes closed, so I could really see him. "There's just . . . always something happening. It never ends. There's never a moment of achievement, finality. Makes you wonder what's the point of it all, always going but never arriving. There's always something else."

"That's life." I said. I wish I hadn't.

7

I found Cull's body just before sunrise. The light was gray, a false dawn showing through the tent. He had used one of his shirts to cover his face. Was that for my sake or his? I said his name a few times.

Clara was furious when I woke her up. She thought I wanted sex, so she kept hitting me and saying no. When she finally heard me she wrapped her arms around my head and I cried in the dark in her chest. She waited for my shock to subside before she said, "How did he die?"

I don't know why I hadn't cut him down. It was the first thing she asked me when we were back in the room looking at him. She was so much better than I am. She should have been me.

"He might still have been breathing when you woke up," she whispered, her hand on his chest.

"He wasn't," I said. He wasn't. He can't have been.

He was so still.

I felt very guilty. Not because I thought his suicide was my fault, not yet anyway, but because I kept thinking that the last thing anyone thought while looking at him was how much they wanted to fuck him. It seemed rude.

The party on our final night down there had been great. We had all had a . . . you know, a "blast." Even with Avon there. We were celebrating her imminent departure from Hecubah, and the new cohort of necromancers and conjurers who were joining us on the Zetland. Cull and I were apprehensive about that, of course. Avon was only too glad to welcome the extra witches into Crysth as long as they weren't on her ship. She said she hadn't any room for civilians, which was nonsense. But what was I supposed to do, call the head Stal a liar? At least we weren't taking any of the mind-control people with us, I can't even imagine what Rhododendron would have said to me if I'd have turned up with mind-control people.

Clara had been charming everyone again. It was her presence that made the party so much fun, the handful of us drinking and talking deep into the night. Neither Cull nor Avon are ever around factionless civilians, so they were showing off, experiencing their own fame through the lens of Clara's amazement. She was playacting of course, she's with me often enough to know that we're all just people. I enjoyed watching her flatter them, lead them to say too much, give themselves away. Jim was there too, infected by the cheekily clandestine mood even though he didn't quite grasp why it existed.

"Do you want to try one?" he said to Clara. I attempted to give her a look which meant "no," but she was still angry that we weren't sleeping in the same room, so she paid me no attention.

She gasped in mock horror and looked at Cull and Avon before saying, "That's far too scary!"

"They're not cold," said Avon, winking as she did. "It's not like you'd expect."

"You've had one?" Cull almost winced at her. He was sitting by her side. Their legs were touching.

"Of course. Wouldn't you?"

"I wouldn't," I said, very firmly, in the hopes that Clara understood that she was forbidden to do so herself.

"Why not?" asked Jim. "They want it."

"Only because you make them want it!" protested Clara. She slapped his arm and he looked at her like he thought he might be able to fuck her rather than one of his dead. Irritating.

"Now now," Avon was using her gravelly voice, so I knew she was about to say something horrible. "If someone were to suffer a sudden, tragic brain aneurism right at the point of orgasm—who are we to deny them an eternity spent in lust?"

I was glad to see that Cull found this as off-putting as I did.

"How do you get the dead people to eat?" asked Clara, brilliantly. She had obviously seen the look on mine and Cull's faces and decided to change the subject before we all got into an argument.

"They don't need to. Our magic supplies the energy, a necromancer is a furnace. And no, it doesn't work on the living. We have tried." Jim lit a cigarette that he had been rolling and then passed it to me. I appreciated that. He'd seen me eyeing it. It wasn't tobacco but it wasn't unpleasant, whatever it was.

"Are they still them?" Cull said.

"What do you mean?" asked Clara, still pretending to be a lot less intelligent than she really was. It worried me sometimes when I saw her doing that. Was she pretending with me, too?

"I mean . . ." Cull focused his attention on her rather than Avon, "Are the dead still themselves in there, or are they just orgasm? Is there anything left of who they were?"

Jim considered this for a moment before saying, "They are who they were. Their desire remains, and it is their particular desire. It still has its own quirks. There will be some who always try to take you in their mouths, others who are violent, passive. Etcetera."

"Perhaps it isn't such a terrible existence, after all," Cull answered. He laughed. Did he mean that? Is that what he wanted? Not the end of being, but the end of the world.

"I think it sounds like a dreadful thing to do to someone," is what I said.

"Pfft," teased Clara, "big important people like you, I bet you've all had to do dreadful things to someone. For the sake of the empire of course."

Avon frowned and then smiled when she realized the barb was aimed at me and not her. There was a sensitivity in her that I did not expect. "Oh? What has Speaker been up to that's so terrible?" she asked.

"Nothing whatsoever," which I shouldn't have said, made me sound guilty of some vague crime I have not committed. Clara was bluffing to make me sound interesting to Avon, I think.

"Oh come on Speaker," said Cull, "spill."

"Nothing, truly."

Avon rolled her eyes. "Boring. What is it about the Red faction which makes you all so dull?"

Responsibility, I almost said, but it would have been childish and untrue. "What about you, Cull?" is what I chose instead. "What's the worst thing you've ever done for Crysth?"

He laughed, "I'm an urban planner! What could I have possibly done? Paved over my fair share of holy sites, I suppose. The locals always hate it but see what happens when we tolerate deities. What about you, commander?"

Avon smiled and pulled a face like she was thinking, sorting through a long list of interplanetary terrorism, I'm sure. "I don't think that anything done in the service of our alliance could be bad," she said. "Our alliance" is definitely what she said. That was a worrying term, and one which had been gaining more traction for a long time. It sounds so commonplace but it frames the empire as existing in four different parts rather than as an inter-reliant monolith. As if Military could detach from the rest of us and be a thing unto itself. I suppose it is, now.

"Oh come on," teased Clara. "There must have been something!"

Avon studied her a while, not unpleasantly, and then said, "Alright. One thing does stick out, I'm not sure why. It was eons ago. I was in the service of my first black hand, the first time I'd ever been deployed. I was young and nervous. Younger than you are now, Clara. And not half as clever, I suspect." I didn't like that obviously, Avon has a reputational fondness for women like Clara, you know. "The planet we were assimilating was on the verge of total war. Our embassy was based in the state which was at fault, a picture-perfect democracy which functioned by hoarding and sapping labor from the rest of the planet's nations." She seemed to reconsider telling us but went on anyway. "The ambassador had us, the Military cohort in his embassy, creeping around at night to slaughter the city's animals. Urban giants. Slow, beautiful, useful to the population. Culturally important, even. They were defenseless, I hated doing it."

I don't know what the hell she was talking about but she should not have said that in front of Jim. He said, "But why?"

She shrugged. "At the time I just obeyed. You do not refuse an order from the black hand. In retrospect, his plan was probably to disrupt the local order, to make the residents realize they were not infallible, turn them against each other to allow doubt into their minds and prevent a global war by provoking introspection." She took a sip of wine. "Didn't work."

It wasn't funny but her delivery made us all laugh. She's actually quite droll, you know.

"Who was it?" asked Cull. "The ambassador."

"Can't remember his name." Both Cull and I balked at the lie. There are, what, seventy black hands in the entire empire at a given time? You don't just forget their names.

Avon was lying all evening. That entire story sounded fake. Cull was on edge about it, I think. It's difficult to tell now whether he was really "on edge" or if I just can't separate anything that happened that night from his death. He seemed fine, jolly even, but then there are flashes of his face or his voice in my memory which now scream to me that he wasn't. Are they real? Yes Ming, it does matter. It matters because I want to know whether or not I could have saved him. If I could, then I hate myself. If I couldn't, then I still hate myself but for different reasons. I would like to cross one off.

He was so heavy. Clara had to cut him down with my seeking knife while I held on to him, and he still fell on top of me even though I was braced for it. She tried chest compressions for a while, but he was gone.

"Get Jim," she said, after we had wrestled him onto his bed.

"No!" I said to her, "Absolutely not."

"Speaker, he can't be dead. Jim can bring him back. He cannot have killed himself down here."

"I know!" I was shriek-whispering, she was calm.

"Then get Jim!"

"No! You don't understand, you heard Jim last night, we'd be reviving him only to . . . he'll be stuck forever, thinking that he wants to die, trying to kill himself over and over until he dies again. Even if we tied him up or something, he'd be stuck feeling like . . ." I inclined my head to the scrap of belt still dangling from the wooden rafter, "*That*. It would be evil."

She put her face in her hands. I was right.

"We need to tell Avon then," is what she said after we had been silent a while. "What if it was one of the brain control people?"

"Are you out of your mind? If she thinks there's trouble while we're down here she won't come. Nobody can know, not yet."

"What? Speaker that's insane, this might have been an assassination!"

"What for!"

"I . . . well what would a suicide be for?"

I kept saying things like, "Everything just needs to be normal." I don't really know what I meant. But it can't have been an assassination, otherwise they would have killed me too.

"Why would they do that?" is what Clara said when I told her this. Which didn't warrant a response.

We got the deodands to help us. We draped Cull's coat over his head and told them that he was drunk, we needed to get him into the ship without the locals seeing him. They knew something was wrong because we wouldn't let them actually touch him, just cover us while we carried him with one arm over each of our shoulders as if he were alive. Perverse.

So, everything that came afterward was my fault. We put him into a medical rig and pretended to hook him up to it. We couldn't really attach him in case it announced that he was dead or communicated something to the techs. I don't know how these things work. That's why he wasn't scanned when the ship ran its de-bugging routine. I just didn't think of it. If only the thing would tell you what it found, make some sort of noise to indicate that you were covered in space mites that it had to zap, then I would have done something. But it doesn't so I just assumed we were fine. Or maybe it does but it only communicates with the technomancers. I don't know. Anyway, my fault. It was all my fault.

We were planning to have dinner together that evening to welcome Avon back into the fold and start making some plans. Just a small affair—the emperors, both stewards, and her. But obviously one of the emperors was dead again and we had a bunch of witches to find quarters for, so there wasn't much of a celebratory mood.

I sent Clara back to my suite and waited for Rhododendron on the landing ship with Cull's body. I should have been there to introduce him to the Hecubans but I was too scared to leave Cull, worried he might be found.

"Speaker." Rhododendron's voice was dangerously low when he came into the ship. I shouldn't say "dangerous." He was never dangerous. Intimidating, sure, but only because of the way he looks. He was never violent. Alright, he was never violent to Crysthians. Adora Ming and Haja came in just after him, and I could tell there were deodands outside the door because they both had their hands held up to instruct them not to enter.

"Rhododendron," I said. "Ambassadors." They nodded at me but did not smile. I remember that because the three of them were just standing there, staring at me. It was unpleasant.

"Speaker," he repeated, forcing me to look at him and notice a shard of metal on his neck glowing insultingly, measuring my pulse or something. "He's got skulls. On his shoes."

"Oh. You mean Jim. I know."

"Speaker. A necromancer."

"I know. I promise that it was necessary. They didn't want Avon to leave, they were scared that the empire would abandon them if we had no connection. They didn't want to lose us." That worked, I knew it would. He's soft, really. "Just think of them as a temporary embassy of Hecubah. And they're deity killers, too."

Adora Ming had obviously noticed Rhododendron relax and was having none of it because she said, "We cannot have unfactioned, extra-imperial civilians fighting our battles for us."

"With us," Haja, shockingly, came to my rescue. "They are extremely powerful, comrade. This unusual beginning to our alliance could be of long-term benefit."

Adora shrugged.

"Look," I began. "Look. We have a huge problem with Cull."

"Good fucking gods," Adora sighed. "What have you done to him?"

She was joking but I couldn't take it. My eyes welled up and I said, "It wasn't me!"

Rhododendron's entire chest lit up then. He always wore the original hammer and sickle necklace for official business, so it would become this horrible shadow in the middle of his glow when he was anxious or annoyed. "What wasn't you? Speaker. Oh fuck. What is 'it'? What have you done?"

"Nothing!"

"It is abundantly clearly not nothing that you have done." Haja was a lot calmer than Rhododendron because black hands always are, but she had a tell in that she would overpronounce her t's when she was angry. She was overpronouncing the fuck out of her t's.

I just said it to get it over with.

There's no way I can remember who said what next without making it up completely. They were all "what"ing and "fuck"ing and "please tell me you are joking"ing. I just kept quiet and opened the door of the medical rig.

Rhododendron was speechless. Adora and Haja were not. I don't know what they were saying, I was just watching Rhododendron.

"You haven't even removed the belt from his neck, Speaker," is what he said, finally. It was almost a whisper.

"It was dark," is all I could manage. "I was in shock."

He started to remove the leather. It was stuck to itself with the weight, but he managed to prize it away.

"Turn around," he ordered, "I need to make sure it's him."

We all looked away, or I did. I don't know if the ambassadors did. I heard Rhododendron sigh.

"Tell me."

I told him everything. Our little nocturnal adventure, Avon's weirdness, Cull's general mood, us having a pleasant time, drinking, then waking up and finding him.

"Adora," is what he said when I had finished. He had this way of saying people's names where it sounded like an instruction, a verb.

"To the remaining Green faction," she had it all ready, there was no pause for thought, "we will tell the truth. Speaker, you will emphasize Cull's strange mood. To everyone else, Cull died aboard the Zetland from unforeseen complications following a heart transplant he received ten years ago. The stress of the situation was overwhelming the organ and, in his eagerness to fulfil his new duties, he did not attend properly to it. Of course, we will clear this narrative with the Greens before we make any announcements."

"The heart transplant, is that true?" Adora nodded to Haja's question. "Excellent. Well done, comrade."

"Don't you dare congratulate yourselves over his body," growled Rhododendron. "Speaker, how can you be certain nobody entered your room? Nobody manipulated him?"

"The deodands were on high alert after we got past them on the first night. They were really slacking you know, just sitting around chatting."

"Get over it, Speaker."

"Over it. But there was nobody else in the room."

"Do witches require proximity?" He asked Haja that for some reason.

"They're already on the ship. We cannot let people know we allowed them onto the ship if we suspect them of murdering the Green emperor." Rhododendron nodded as Haja spoke. "Can you imagine?"

"Good point," Adora agreed. "Tell the Greens that Avon definitely had the area secured."

Rhododendron nodded again and then glared at me. The ambassadors joined in.

"What?" I asked, "What do you want me to have done?"

Rhododendron sighed and Haja patted him on the shoulder, which was annoying. I was the one who found a dead man and had to drag him through a witch-infested swamp. Where was my pat? Anyway that's when I learned that everything was much worse than it seemed.

"I'm sorry," he said to me. "Things have not been going well here, either. This is poor timing."

"I'm not sure there's good timing for a suicide," mused Adora. "Unless it's your own of course."

"Shut up," he ordered, casually. "We've had some more incidents of the Apechi virus. Don't panic. I said don't. It doesn't look like another attack, it just appears limited to the people who were close to Juniper when she died."

"Oh no. Oh no. What about us?"

"You'd know if you were afflicted. It causes . . . growths."

"Oh no."

"Indeed." Haja said. "We've quarantined of course, but there doesn't seem to be anything we can do for them. Some have died already. Poor Greens."

"What do they die of? Like Juniper?" I asked.

Rhododendron shook his head. "Not as spectacularly as Juniper, but yes in the same way. The deity causes spines to develop on the bones of the afflicted. The spines keep growing indefinitely, the victims succumb to internal bleeding. All we could do was make them unafraid."

"The good news is that it does seem to be contained to those initially exposed. It isn't, for the time being, spreading." Adora looked at Cull's body. "I wonder if it had anything to do with this? Those afflicted have reported strange visions, compulsions . . ."

"It will certainly make his death easier to explain."

"Haja, I must say that I do not like the way this narrative is developing." It's terrible to argue over a corpse but I really was getting annoyed. "It sounds like you all think this was my fault. We don't need to 'explain' anything, we have the truth."

She said, "I fear sometimes that the truth may not be very useful."

"Agreed," said Adora. "Now can we stop talking like we're being recorded?"

Telling the Greens about Cull wasn't as bad as it could have been. Rhododendron was excellent, I was a mess of course but it would have been inappropriate not to be. They were all just quiet, in shock, I think—either that or they wanted us to leave before they revealed otherwise. If it was the latter then I'm very grateful, I couldn't have coped with it in any other way.

We all decided to spend that evening together in Vard's suite with Avon, leave the Greens alone, the witches to settle, and avoid formality while we mourned. Of course we didn't really have time or energy for mourning. Grief is an exhausting performance and we'd only just stopped doing it for Juniper.

Funnily enough, that evening was actually the first time I'd ever been into the Military residential wing. It's exactly how you'd imagine, weapons all over the walls, gravity suits, strange ancient armor, slogans everywhere. That's why Ella's holed up in there now I suppose, he has an endless supply of things to hit you with.

Vard's suite revealed an interesting taste in interior design. Actually, I can't really imagine Vard picking out a sofa, so surely it had to be someone else's taste—but it was extremely minimalistic. All beige and white with soft edges, like the room and all its contents had been formed out of the same clay. Easygoing and austere at the same time.

Avon had dropped the Avon act. She wasn't even wearing her wig, just lying on his sofa staring at the ceiling, grunting and sitting up occasionally to sip whiskey through a straw. Neat whiskey, mind you. Through a straw.

We were all subdued. Everything was going wrong. Again. Or, continuing to go wrong at an accelerating pace. Which is funny because I would die to go back to that evening now. I wasn't happy, but those were the last moments before complete and total hell. No offense.

It was Rhododendron who broke the silence. He said: "Vard, what is this one?" Vard disentangled himself from Daksha and went over to him, standing at this big cabinet with swords and guns and all that frippery.

Daksha rolled her eyes at me, which was nice. We were surrounded by people whose idea of a good time was a fistfight. It was nice to be recognized as more like her than like them.

"Ahhh." Vard had such a delighted tone of voice that we all looked over. It was the first note of levity we had heard all evening. "This is one of the first target locking blades ever made. It doesn't quite work. Disengages and reengages every time you turn it. However, that makes it good to train with because you have to fight your weapon as well as your opponent."

Avon sat up at that. "Let me have a go."

"It looks far too heavy," mused Daksha, standing to walk over to them. I followed.

"Not for these old bones." Avon smiled as Rhododendron handed it over. "Oh yes, it's terrible. What an antique."

She swung it around and glanced it off Vard's arm in a playful sort of way. Daksha fussed over him as if it could possibly have scratched his dermal armor.

"I'll take the winner," Vard said, looking at Rhododendron and nodding to the cabinet.

Ella clapped. "Speaker, I've got a bottle of Muhr spirit on Avon winning."

"You're on." I knew full well I would lose but I couldn't very well say so, could I?

Rhododendron surveyed the cabinet.

"But isn't Avon at an unfair disadvantage with that old sword?" asked Daksha.

"Ha!" was Avon's response.

"What are all these swords even for?" I asked, to take the pressure off Rhododendron while he chose. "Just exercises?"

"Oh you know we come across all sorts of beasts," Avon answered, still slashing around with the blade, which looked absurdly large in her tiny creep hands. She must have gravity assist or something, who knows. "Then there are certain environments you can't shoot in, and there are always unnatural things which demand a personal touch."

"What, you're really still out there having sword fights?" Daksha smiled. "I don't believe it. You just want to play with knives."

"While I plead guilty to wanting to play with knives, we do end up in sword fights every now and then," said Vard, filling our glasses. "Not even always because we're in an uncooperative environment or battling something unreal, sometimes it's just the right thing to do."

"What on earth does that mean?" she asked him.

"Oooh, I have a good one here." Ella flourished into the conversation in the way he does. "We once landed on one of Celia's moons because the deimancers were getting a strong signal from over there. Turns out it was a monstrosity the local kingdom or whathaveyou was thinking of as a god of war. We explained our deicidal intent and instead of complaining they said they thought this was fair enough as long as I could best the brute in single combat. So we have a choice, nuke or sword fight. Civilization is in the blade, darlings!"

"Don't you have to destroy everything a deity was a part of in order to kill it, though?" I asked.

"Nope," said Avon. "In fact you can't kill them at all—they're not real. You can only stop them from moving. They spread without multiplying, but they need conscious attention in order to do so." Her eyes went glassy for a moment, then she swung the blade again and carried on in a lighter voice. "Which suggests to me that consciousness isn't real either. But the point is that you can only stop them from being able to move. Understand?"

"Exactly," grinned Ella, "so the moment I taught that hairy little beast how to dance, all its supplicants thought no more of it. Now the poor darling's stuck wherever they get stuck when there's nobody to look at them."

"You fought a deity in single combat?" asked Rhododendron, turning around with a scimitar in his hands.

"Good choice," said Avon.

"Now you mention it, Ella, I actually know that story already." Daksha's voice was stern. "You have told it many times in the Ethicist wing, apparently. It got back to me from some of the ladies. And by some, I mean many."

Ella simpered. "Forgive me, darling Daksha, but if a man can't use a duel with a god to gain a brief advantage where beautiful women are concerned then what's the point of anything?"

I laughed, unfortunately. It was funny. So did Vard though.

Daksha was unamused. "You are one squabble away from getting yourself banned."

"They *fight* over me?" He grinned with all of his teeth, "Tell me everything!"

"Not endearing, Ella," Rhododendron grumbled, then leveled the scimitar in Avon's direction. "Come on then."

It was fun watching Rhododendron get his ass handed to him by Avon. A buffalo bested by a mouse. Well that's not fair. They were both great about it, she started giving him tips and he hit her a couple of times. I never sorted out the bet with Ella because Vard joined in too soon. Plus, it was quite obvious that Avon was trying not to properly hit Rhododendron in case she hurt him, whereas he could assume she was completely covered in armor and whack at will. She broke a sweat trying to keep him and Vard away. They got her to yield eventually, still laughing.

It was when we were all sitting back in the lounge area that things went worse. We were talking about Avon's potential plans for the future, but only abstractly as she had made it quite clear that she was unwilling to go into detail until she and Vard had some time alone.

Daksha was saying something about keeping the medics who had treated those infected by the Apechi virus in quarantine for the next few months when Avon interrupted.

"Don't move," she said.

"Excuse me?"

Avon was staring at Daksha's chest, her head still as she unfolded the rest of her body from the chair. It was a really strange movement, you could tell that she was engaging augmented joints, bringing her bioware to life. "Don't move. Daksha, don't worry, don't move."

"Wait, what is that?" said Ella.

"What is what?" breathed Daksha.

I saw it too. A hole in Daksha's chest, about a thumbnail in size. It was tiny but it moved with your eyes so that no matter which angle you viewed her from, you could still see the chair behind her.

"Suboptimal," said Rhododendron.

"What is suboptimal? What are you all looking at?"

"Stay still, my love."

"Vard. You're all scaring me."

"I feel like she should be scared." suggested Ella, earning a punch in the arm from Vard which obviously deadened it.

"It's a witch mite," said Avon, who had removed her sweater and was balling it up with intent, "A pest from Hecubah. Must have sneaked onto your landing ship. It will feel like it's harming you but it isn't, it's just pain."

"What?"

"I feel like pain is harm," said Ella, unperturbable.

Then Daksha yelped, slapping her hands over her ears. Avon jumped for her at the same time, trying to gather the thing into her sweater and yelling at Daksha to be still.

"Fuck!" Avon straightened up, looking for something in the fabric which obviously wasn't there. "If there's one there's another. Look around."

"Avon," said Rhododendron, verbishly.

She made a noise of defeat and said, "They're just mites. They don't hurt us they—"

"That hurt so much!"

"It's just in your head, it isn't real. They're in the same space the Hecubans' magic comes from. We caught a bunch but they die very quickly in captivity. We think they might even be the source of the magic, you can only see them when they're on flesh. There!" she pointed at Rhododendron.

He looked at the hole in his arm with a very Rhododendron expression. Resignation and curiosity.

"You brought a pest back with you from Hecubah?" Vard said to me. "How?"

Ella scoffed. "Well done, Speaker."

"How do you know it was me and not Avon!"

"Speaker, you know it was you," said Rhododendron, allowing Avon to wrap his arm in sweater. "Did you catch it?"

"I have no idea if this even works." She looked around as if for a cup and a magazine. "Ella, call my techs. This is great."

"What do you mean 'great'? That was awful!" Vard had arranged himself around Daksha but she was taking no comfort in it. "Speaker, what the hell!"

"Why does everybody assume this was me!"

"It damn well was you, you better—" Then Rhododendron grimaced and doubled over in pain, his chest lighting up and his eyes closed tight.

"See! See!" shouted Daksha, vindicated by his agony.

"Ella, call Avon's techs!" Vard commanded.

"How?!"

Daksha was still protesting, "What for? Kill it!"

"No no you don't understand, if we can work out what they are we might get control of the magic, I've been trying to catch them for ages. There!"

8

Speaker stopped talking, looked toward the door.

"What?" Ming, opening her eyes at the silence. "Is Xar back?"

"Yes. Should I leave? He . . . won't like that I'm in here." Speaker could not hear the Apechi general but they could sense him; godmagic disturbs the air in such a way that the afflicted can feel its presence.

She allowed cruelty to slit a smile across her face before she asked, "Scared?"

"Of course."

The door opened, and in came Xar Kis.

He is the leader of Apech, its spearhead and tyrant. Their god appears to love him like nobody else. He is possessed of its impossible strength and foresight. Before he met Ming he had been confined to Lon Apech, a tiny city with no future that he could see. He invaded Crysth beside her solely for the freedom its ships afford him.

"What," he drawled, "is going on in here?" His one eye fell on Speaker's back, the papers around them, then up to Ming's smirk. "Get out."

"Me?" Speaker squeaked, not turning to look at him.

"Do you think," answered Xar, the sound of his boots drawing closer to Speaker's chair as he spoke, "there is any chance whatsoever that I meant Ming?"

Speaker clutched a few of their papers and hurried for the door. On the other side of it, they began to scream.

Ming looked at Xar questioningly, to which he replied: "I brought you a little gift, Speaker's just being hysterical about it."

She extended a beckoning hand to him over the side of the tub, "Have you been in the Military wing this whole time?"

"No, I—" He paused midway through unbuttoning his shirt, "Have you been drinking?" His eye caught the other glass. "With Speaker?"

"They're a better storyteller when they're relaxed." She sighed. "Get in."

"Better storyteller."

"Don't you repeat me," she said as he slipped into the tub beside her, "that's my trick."

He removed the eyepatch over the wreck of his left eye, put his arms around her as she explored it with her tongue. She could feel that he had not relaxed, that there was something on his mind. She waited for him to tell her.

"I can't get Ella out of the Military wing without killing more Crysthians." He sounded tired, which he was. He wanted power only, to slide into the thrones of Crysth while leaving the empire intact. The state of the Zetland was testament to how badly this was going; not only did he have no control over the magic he used to force Crysth's surrender, but there was still a pocket of Crysthian rebels in the palace who refused to accept it.

"We'll just have to starve them out, then."

"We will be waiting a very long time. They're as well fed in there as we are in here."

"I didn't realize we were in a hurry." She cocked her head to the side as she said this, searching his face for clues. He is important to her, but she can't always tell what he wants.

"No, there is no hurry. But I am impatient. You are too, don't pretend. I've been waiting all my life to get away from Apech, and now I'm stuck somewhere else. You do know that those of them still resisting our take-over will never obey us? Even when we win."

"Yes, but it isn't about them. We can't be emperors with a staff which hates us. We need everyone on the Zetland to see that we don't want to hurt the . . . rebels. That we are trying to reason with them."

"But I do want to hurt them. Very much so in fact."

"We'll get them eventually, just not at this critical juncture, not while we're taking charge."

"Who knew that taking over an empire would be so boring."

"At least you get to fight. I'm stuck in here with Speaker."

"Find anything?"

"What do you think? Do I look infected to you?"

He opened his eye, surveyed her mutilated face. He would be able to tell immediately if his god had decided to take her. "You look beautiful. Where were you in the story?"

"Mite invasion."

Xar laughed, "I like that part. Speaker's a fucking idiot."

"Want to listen? It's almost relaxing now I gave them time to think about it and get everything in the right order. More like a narrative than a panic attack, at least." She licked his cheek and something on it activated her antibacterial device.

He pushed her and her crown of foul-tasting mist away before saying, "Only if we can skip to Vard's . . . incident. I still don't like the position his death puts me in. Access to the library is going to be blocked for a lot longer. The godbeasts are congregating around there, it's hard to fight when they are so many of them."

"I don't think Speaker's lying, they would have cracked by now."

"I don't think they're lying either but I will be relieved when I see Vard with my own eyes."

"Eye."

He glared at her in a monocular way.

"Don't be like that, you know I think you look better now." She pushed a button at the tub's side. "Speaker, come back in here."

A noise materialized. A mix of heartrending despair and "um."

"What did you do, what's upsetting Speaker?" she asked.

The door opened again, "He's dying." Speaker's voice shook.

"Who is?" asked Ming.

Xar did a dismissive wave of his hand, "He was dying anyway. Brain tumor, it's for Ming."

Ming had developed an obsession with all growths, malignant or otherwise. She never articulates it to herself in this way but she believes, somewhere, that she can force the Apechi deity to notice her by imbibing deformity, inscribing it into her flesh. It modifies the bodies of the anointed and she hurts herself to show that she is willing to change. To lure its infection into her, have it warp her bones. It doesn't care.

Speaker said, "I know him. He's a good man."

"Ask a guard to end his suffering if it's bothering you."

"What a bore," said Ming.

"Total bore," agreed Xar.

Speaker reappeared. "What do you want from me?"

"I don't like your tone," said Xar, earning him a subaquatic squeeze of warning from the woman in his lap.

"What does it matter?" Speaker knelt on the chaise longue, head bowed.

"Oh come now, don't be depressed as well as be Speaker. It's unbearable." Ming.

"What's wrong with you?" Xar.

Speaker looked up at them both, mouth slightly open. "He was a nice man."

Xar rolled his eye before saying, "A nice man with a brain tumor. Brain tumor. Killing him was charity. You did a good thing."

"He had no tongue."

Ming frowned at Xar. "You can't publicly torture civilians when we're trying to pretend to do a peaceful occupation."

"Nobody saw me," he said. "It was for his own good anyway. He was babbling, begging, embarrassing himself. If it were me I would much rather my last words were silence."

Speaker stared.

"Benevolence." Xar.

Ming laughed. Speaker did not.

"Oh lighten up. Xar wants to hear about Vard again."

"I wasn't there. You know I wasn't there."

"You were more there than we were," said Ming.

"Did you see for a fact that he isn't in control of himself anymore?" asked Xar.

An expression neither of the two invaders had ever seen before appeared momentarily on Speaker's lips before they parted to ask, "Why, you scared?"

Ming's breath caught in her throat. She looked between Xar and Speaker, pressed her hands hard on Xar's chest. Useless, she wouldn't be able to hold him if he decided to get up and smash Speaker to pieces.

But Xar was bored, too. Resistance from Speaker therefore seemed like a new avenue of entertainment rather than a birthplace of uncontrollable rage. "Of Vard? Yes, Speaker, I am scared of Vard. Very scared in fact." He laughed and leaned his head back against the tub. "Your brother caused me enough trouble. You're more fun when you're drunk."

This last line made Ming look at Xar in an empty, reckoning way she has when she doesn't quite understand him. She will never see it but there is a part of Xar Kis that craves Speaker's approval. Not out of personal respect, but out of desire to be accepted as part of Crysth's empire. Speaker's loyalty would mean that it was right that Xar had taken a throne, would make him a successor rather than a usurper. Ming will never understand this because she is marinaded in certainty. She is so thoroughly a part of the imperial core that she cannot imagine what it is like to be without it; the constant and blinding self-assurance of having been born in the center. She could not think outside Crysth's terms even as she orchestrated its demise.

"I've seen enough to know that he isn't Vard anymore," Speaker began. "He would never. He hit Daksha, remember. He just would never."

"So your only evidence that Vard is not Vard is, what, a bit of domestic abuse?" Xar likes to be told, again and again, that he doesn't have to fear the dead emperor.

"And Rhododendron," Speaker almost whispered. "But Daksha should be enough. Vard would never hurt her."

"I'm sure," began Ming, "that you would have once said the same about yourself."

Speaker's gaze flicked guiltily over to a mirror in the corner of the room. It had been smashed, its broken pieces were gone.

"Well?" Ming said. "Carry on."

9

I only know by coincidence. Everyone else still thinks Vard's alive, or, they did before you arrived. Ella may have told them by now.

I was in Avon's office with Haja and Rhododendron. Just another Military room which Vard had loaned to her. Avon was explaining that she wanted to get us to someone who can perceive deities. Like a deimancer, but not like ours. Someone who understood what we call "deities" as actual gods rather than as problems of physics. Rhododendron didn't like it, said it was like walking into a viper's nest for help with a snake problem. Haja said that a viper's nest was the best place for help with a snake problem, so we ended up arguing about snakes for a while.

"They have the same diet, it would be in their interest to get rid of the competing species. There are only so many mice to go around," Haja said.

"But we are the mice, you realize that we are the mice in this analogy." countered Rhododendron.

Avon pursed her lips. "Are we? I feel like it would be more apt to think of space as mice."

"Yes," agreed Haja. "Go on."

"If the unnatural entity can be thought of as 'wanting' anything, then it is expansion. All they do is get bigger. We are incidental to them."

"No, we are instrumental to them. They operate through us. They *infect* us. We are space. Are you both forgetting what's going on here?"

"Don't be sarcastic," snapped Haja. "We do not know enough about these entities to—"

"Exactly!" Avon slapped her palm on the table in front of her, "We do not know. We destroy these things wherever we find them—and with damn good reason, yes, they are unpredictable sources of uncontrollable power that do not adhere to the laws of reality as we know them, therefore—"

"Oh just some *unpredictable sources of uncontrollable power that do not adhere to the laws of reality as we know them*." Rhododendron imitated her voice. "Can you hear yourself?"

"Rhododendron, I do not mean to understate how dangerous they can be. I am simply trying not to understate how little we know about them. We aren't even agreed on what they are! What I am saying is that we need to go to someone who has a better idea."

"Yes," Haja nodded, "to defeat the viper, we need to get inside its mind."

"It isn't a viper, it doesn't have a mind!"

"I must say," I chipped in, "I feel this metaphor has reached the end of its utility. Although if we could all suspend our disbelief it could be useful in a sort of socialist surrealist way—"

"Speaker. On our mother's corpse, if you start banging on about socialist surrealism then I am going to start stuffing pieces of you back into it."

I did consider pointing out that this was an excellent example of socialist surrealism but thought better of it.

That was when there was the knocking. We all knew knocking was trouble, nobody would ever interrupt a meeting between a general and an emperor in normal circumstances. It had been happening a lot in those days, obviously, but it was still bad. What the fuck is it now. Witch mites in the hospital, flame bear rampage in the gardens, etcetera.

It was two Military captains come to find Avon. They were both sweating, with expressions like we were all about to die.

"It's Vard," said one of them, a Muhr with a voice box. "We don't know what's happened. We've apprehended the necromancer, but we don't know what's happened. You need to come. Ella's there."

"Which one of the necromancers? Skull Shoes?" I avoided Rhododendron's face when she nodded. Everybody had decided that Jim was my fault. "What has he done?"

"We don't know. Please come."

We shut down traffic so that we could get there immediately. Rhododendron hadn't wanted to, in case it made people panic, but the captains were really insisting. It was only for a few minutes but everyone always notices. I hate using the walls, I manage to forget most of the time that there are technomancers lurking in there. That the ship is flesh and metal as well as they are and they're in there just . . . flying around. But what can you do?

When we arrived in the library, I had the sense that nobody had moved since the captains left to fetch us. Such a bizarre scene. I should paint it, in oils or acrylic perhaps. Maybe even an ink painting, like an ironic landscape. It was a mess, books everywhere and tables singed. There'd been fire, explosions. Ella was kneeling on Jim, who looked like he didn't need to be restrained. There were other Hecubans too but they weren't trying to help him. Daksha was sitting in the middle of the mess, surrounded by Ethicists. She was so still, I'm not exaggerating when I say that for a moment I thought she wasn't her but just a paused holo. It was as if she had shut down while she waited to be told it hadn't happened, or that it could be undone. Her chin was bleeding where Vard had struck her.

"What happened?" Avon demanded, "Ella. Where is Vard?"

Ella swallowed and shook his head. "The, oh . . . darling."

"And where are all the mites?" Avon asked again. She had wanted to herd them into one space, somewhere large and vacant enough that they wouldn't die or bother anyone. The library had been the only real choice.

"Still in here," offered a Hecuban I recognized as the lead conjurer, in the weird tones of the translator they were wearing. "We were . . . we managed to corner a swarm but our conjurings got out of hand."

"Out of hand?!" shrieked Ella, waving his arm around at the steaming chaos which had been the library. "Behold, darlings, 'out of hand'!"

"Vard was worried that they were going to destroy our records . . ." murmured one of the captains. "He got in their way. It . . . was very clearly an accident."

"What was?" whispered Rhododendron.

"No." Avon's voice was firm. Like she thought that if she denied what we knew was coming with enough force then it would cease to do so out of deference to her rank. "No, no."

"Avon, do something!" Ella gestured farther into the library, so we followed her in the direction of his finger.

We heard Vard before we saw him. He was humming to himself. Perverse.

He'd taken off his shirt and was using it to flap at the embers. Picking up books and dusting them off, piling them onto the tables. Bustling. I can't describe it. It was so wrong. Like he was acting.

"Vard?" asked Avon. He ignored her and kept humming.

"What's happening?" Rhododendron stepped forward. "Vard? Vard."

He ignored Rhododendron.

"Oh, gods," is what I said.

"He was protecting the books when he died," is what Avon said. She was the first to realize what happened, of course.

"Oh, gods." I could only repeat myself.

My brother said my name, as if this was my fault too. I hope it wasn't.

"Rho, stand back." Avon slid around the table to Vard's side, trying to get in his face. He could not or would not see her. She closed her eyes, looked at me kind of like she wanted me to stop her, and picked up a book.

The blast knocked her off her feet, sent her flying across the room. I don't even know what it was, some sort of . . . I don't know, I'll only be making it up. Some air cannon in Vard's bioware but she *flew*. He ran after her, still humming but louder and threatening. Have you ever heard someone hum in a threatening way? Fucking terrifying. But she'd already figured it out so she got to her feet and threw the book back at him. He caught it and cradled it, then started to ignore her again.

Rhododendron was having Rhododenrony hysterics. Shouting meaningless orders at everyone which they were all trying and failing to obey. Ella eventually managed to drag Jim over, but the translator couldn't keep up with how quickly he was talking so it was a total mess.

"Is he dead? Is he fucking *dead*?!" yelled Avon, knowing it to be so.

Jim nodded.

"Bring him back!" I've never heard Rhododendron afraid before. No, yes I have. When our mother died, he was afraid. But we'd been ready for that and not for Vard, who he worshipped.

We were ten or eleven when Vard was crowned. He wore his hair in long braids down his back with Military blue beads woven in for the occasion. Mother got us both guns a bit like his to play with. I had no idea what I was supposed to do with mine so Rhododendron appropriated it and spent a year shooting holes in my canvases. Mother wouldn't stop him, she told me that my patience would make me better now, and his guilt would make him better later. She was probably right.

Anyway I was trying to be the reasonable one so I said, "He can't."

"What do you mean he *can't*? He's right there!"

"Yes, but he's dead!"

"Well then we must have vastly different ideas of the concept of death!"

"Oh shut the fuck up!" yelled Ella. "Who asked Hammer and Sickle to come in here?! This is Military business! Make this motherfucker make some sense." He shook Jim in front of him to indicate that he was the motherfucker.

"What, what the fuck did you just call us?" demanded Rhododendron, coming to himself.

"Which of us is Hammer and which is Sickle?" I asked. I still don't know. Rude.

"Jim." Daksha's voice cut through the room. We all turned to her. She still had that expression like the world had already ended. She was letting the blood ruin her suit. "Is he really gone? Is it over?"

We waited for the translator to speak to him, to speak to us.

"Yes. I'm sorry."

*

"So, dead Vard can still use his bioware." Xar Kis opened his eye and fixed it on Ming. "I don't like that at all."

"Oh, *now* we can interrupt?" She stood from the water and began to knock suds from her body with a flounce of irritation. "Speaker, go back to what Avon was saying about gods and physics. What did she mean about that? She knows stuff."

"No," broke in Kis. "It's my turn, let's get some actually useful information." He whispers when he's angry. "I need to know about Vard."

"What more is there?" Ming climbed out of the tub and over to her clothes. "His mind's gone. He only protects the books."

"I'm going to have to fight him at some point, you are being—"

"I don't see why." They both turned to look at Speaker, surprised by the interruption. "Pardon me, I just . . . I don't see why you're going to have to fight him. Vard won't leave the library. He didn't even recognize Daksha, I keep saying. He's gone. There's really no reason for you to fight him, unless you want a book." Speaker had been able to hear their whispered little bickerings throughout the whole story and, lubricated by half a bottle of wine, had decided to mediate.

"See." Ming punctuated the word with a click as she fixed a palm-sized black rectangle to the mechanism behind her ear. Once secured, it unfurled into a series of curved triangles which knitted together over her face to obscure its mutilation. The mask rippled into the shape of her lips, even her dimpled chin, then settled into a cold metallic stasis which suited her as much as the debris of flesh beneath.

Kis watched Speaker for a while then said, "If you are wrong, I will treat the mistake as a betrayal."

"Speaker cannot betray you. Speaker isn't on your side." Ming.

Kis smiled, loving her but just a little, waiting for whatever she was going to say.

Speaker saw the Red in her then. That is what she had been, before she was this. A trainee in the ranks, on her way to getting her own set of black hands. She had the diplomat's habit of saying clever-sounding nothing-meaning declarations of something. It's supposed to throw you off while they work out what they're really doing.

"Or do you disagree with me?" she whispered to Speaker. "Do you think you're us?"

The radio burst into life before Speaker knew how to respond.

"Sir." A man's voice with a Crysthian accent. "Do you still want us to escort you all to medical?"

Ming stood, thrusting the glass back into Speaker's hand. "We're through to the medical wing? Why didn't you say so? We've wasted all this time."

"Can't a man even have a bath around here?"

"Come with me or don't." The door creaked shut behind her.

And then Speaker found themself alone with Xar Kis. A day full of surprises. It's tough to say which of the pair Speaker loathes more, but they consider Kis somewhat redeemable because he is a foreigner. He is from a planet beyond Crysth's empire, and therefore obviously cannot quite help his violent impulses.

"Would you like me to continue with the story?" Speaker asked.

Xar chuckled in his soft, empty way before saying, "Go and tell her to wait for me. Are you coming with us?"

10

This is what had become of the Zetland.

The Military quadrant—where Ella governed a few hundred Crysthians still loyal to the fight against Apech—remained relatively sane. They squirmed, they plotted, they fought. It might have been going better for Ella if they were actually all soldiers, or if his enemy made sense.

The Apechi invaders brought their god with them, wielding but not understanding its strength. The sacrosanct can see reactions, possibilities, conditions; their flesh can sneak around time and choose to ignore the blade thrust into it. But this vision torments them also, shows them lies that send them to their deaths. They have learned to not quite trust their god. The skin of the anointed blurs with potentiality, broils and rolls with all the movement it could have made. To their eyes those unafflicted are still, quiet, peaceful.

But Avon Stal was right, Apech could not meet Crysth in plain combat despite their unnatural advantages. They had hijacked the ship, which was not a power to be underestimated. They could, theoretically, drop everybody within it dead. This would not look good; they were trying to take, not exterminate. However, neither the Apechi crusaders nor the Crysthian rebels were the worst of the Zetland's disorders.

Apech's allies swarmed the palace. They were weak and pathetic but a patchwork of horror nonetheless. They were not willing allies. They weren't truly real; avatars of what Crysth likes to call "deities." But they were unlike Apech's raging, vibrant, pulsing god—more like memories of what they could have been had they been allowed to develop. Incarnations, dolls. Xar Kis spent most of his time trying to clear them rather than Ella's rebels from the ship.

A cloud of air was sucked through a metal mask, enjoyed, and exhaled.

"You're glad to be out of Speaker's apartment, I take it?" Kis held Ming's wrist to his chest as he watched the uncovered portion of her face, heard her breath rattle beneath her mask. He enjoyed her enjoyment.

"Ecstatic." she whispered, and then they were walking.

Their progress was decorated with guilt. Soldiers in Crysthian uniforms stood to attention for the invaders and avoided Speaker's gaze.

There were Apechi guards in every corridor. They waved in open delight to see Ming, who ignored them. She was a talisman to them as much as she was a leader.

Her hands matched her mask—contoured black gloves mimicking the reptile-topographied prosthetics of Red ambassadors. She wore a Red uniform. She did so because she knew that those who surrendered to her comforted themselves with the thought of her status and her name. She was one of them—Crysthian, valid, an authority. It wasn't a surrender, just a change of management.

She knew that Speaker's presence behind her had the same legitimizing effect as her ersatz black hands. Speaker did not.

"What was that?" she asked, waving in the direction of an orange stain on the ceiling but not breaking her stride.

"A tedium. It was a kind of hexagon." Xar.

Speaker sped up and, exhilarated by their first venture into the Zetland in months, asked, "A kind of hexagon?"

"There's no better way to put it." Kis was pleased by the interest. "It turned anyone or anything that touched it into the loveliest shade of orange. We managed to pop it like a grape by touching it with a spear which was *already* orange. Took ages to mix the right shade."

Speaker's face showcased a progression through the stages of ontological horror until it reached acceptance before they said, "Clever."

"One of my particular favorites," Kis said, slowing down slightly, "was musical. It was just a symphony of noise like birdsong, sirens. Things like the sound of weapons being drawn. We were going to just leave it there but it started repeating things which we had said, bleating for attention in our rather incriminating voices. We rid ourselves of that one by trapping it in a little soundproof case. I still have it."

"Fascinating," Speaker said, referring not to the existence of a dying musical god but the fact that Xar Kis had kept it.

The medical wing was clear of the unnaturals, but not yet the evidence of having fought them. Its walls had been baptized with blood, grease, hair. Mutilated metal, coral growing from joints in the doors. Crysthians mixed with Apechi as they discussed ways to remove the weirdest of it. Speaker watched them, noticed the invaders beginning to dress more like the invaded, noticed the latter's lack of fear. These soldiers started off as enemies but now they had fought gods together, were beginning to accept that they were on the same side. Resentment spiked in Speaker's chest but so did relief.

Almost everyone within the restricted part of the medical wing had a mechanical jaw. Some of them glared sullenly at the invaders, most carried on with whatever they were doing already. The techs or "technomancers" considered themselves above and beyond such trivial matters as governance. They had the secrets of the universe to contend with.

"The best way," began one of them in an unwaveringly authoritative confidence, "to get this information you want is just by watchin' the holos. None of youse are gonna reckon much o' the raw info here, you get me? But you can watch the emperors bein' briefed. Nothin' Speaker hasn' already heard though."

Xar gave Ming a "told you so" twitch of the lip before holding his hand out for the technomancer to lead the way. He was very fond of the gear-faced techs, excited both by the knowledge they represented and their characteristic disregard for authority.

Following, lost, a stranger in a familiar place, Speaker began to panic. The warmth drained from their face. They could feel their pulse in their neck. Watching the holo meant seeing the emperors, facing Rhododendron. The steward steadied themself on the side of a desk, feeling their hands begin to seize in panic around its edge, and waited for the room to darken.

Holograms are duller than life. Crysthian civilians were not used to being photographed or recorded at all, but watching a photorealistic, life-size version of yourself would unnerve anyone. In an effort to lessen the raw freakiness of the experience, the holos were made strange. They were rendered as glowing things which blurred the features and forgave subtle movements. They could not be sent or transferred and played only in the room which recorded them. This was ostensibly for individual privacy and to prevent fakes, but really so that the state's follies could not be broadcast. Speaker's eyes fell on their brother as his image flickered into the room.

Rhododendron towered, arms folded, shoulders hunched in the way of very large men who are trying not to loom. Beside him stood Vard, his hand resting on a pistol he did not need. Speaker tore their eyes away from Rhododendron.

Xar walked straight over to the glowing not-Speaker. He was shorter than the holo in its pointed, high-heeled boots. The two Speakers in the room were nothing alike. The past version stood with its hands clasped behind its back, a slight lean to one side, its jaw lifted. A permanently raised eyebrow gave its face a look of haughty curiosity dissected by horizontal lines of golden henna. Waist-length hair lay shining with glitter down its back.

The real Speaker trembled. Hollow, tiny, hating the vision of themself.

"Speaker," a flirtation in Xar Kis's voice. "You were *pretty*. I'd be much nicer to you if you were still pretty. Why don't you do your hair like that? Look, your fingernails have patterns on them. Can you put patterns on my fingernails?"

Almost panting with the effort of suppressing a panic attack Speaker answered, "I would need to wash my hair, to do it like that. You have to let me into the bathroom."

"Well wash it then." Kis's thumb crossed the impalpable border of the hologram's nose. "Pretty."

Once Xar had finished with Speaker, he went on to poke the ghostly Vard in hopes that the lie contained clues about the man.

"What is Daksha wearing?" he asked after a while.

In shallow gasps Speaker answered, "Alo-Grimm."

"What? And what's the matter with you?"

"Her shoes. The designer's name is Alo-Grimm." They reeled again slightly as they looked back toward their own image. "Same as my jacket."

"If you're having a heart attack, I am not resuscitating you. And I meant in her face, not her clothes. She doesn't have these piercings on the banner pictures of her."

Ming stalked over to inspect the Ethicist emperor's holo. "I think the piercings are disguising dermal implants. Translators?"

"I don't know." Speaker.

"We need to find out," Ming said. "It might be something we can track her with."

"Where are Ella and Avon Stal?" Kis.

"Playing with the microscopes, over there." Ming.

In the corner of the room, the technomancer cleared his throat. "Youse ready for me to hit go or what?"

Eternally delighted by the insolence of the gear-faced wizards, Xar said, "Hit away."

The light dimmed.

"Some puzzling duality has emerged as far as the psychological symptoms are concerned." A technician with a heavily tattooed face and hands emerged into the holo's catch area to stand before Rhododendron. "About half the people it infects it just devastates their brains. Ravages them, they don't know who they are, can't really talk. But then the other half report a strong sense of déjà vu, followed by flashes of dreamlike visions about events in the near future. We don't know what its criteria are, but it does seem to discard some people and take hold of others."

Avon's ghost lurked through Xar Kis before she said, "The god shows people the future?"

The tech shook his head. "The events the infected describe do not always transpire. In fact I would hazard that the dreams are more a reflection of the dreamer's anxiety than the deity itself were it not for the occasional validation. Small stuff—the ability to predict under which cup I have placed a ball, to catch it with their eyes closed. Many of them tried to refuse to get into the pods." At this point the tech tensed, glanced over his shoulder at some unseen sin. "They believed that they knew what . . . was going to happen to them. Some went peacefully. For the same reason."

Rhododendron's face crumpled for a second. Then he said, "They're at peace, now."

"Completely," agreed the tech. "The drugs have made them forget all of this. They will fade out in joy and ignorance."

"It's not right," Daksha broke in. "People deserve to know that they are dying. We do not have the right to take knowledge away from them."

"In normal circumstances I would agree." Another technician's voice came from somewhere at the room's edge. "But we needed to isolate them as quickly as possible. And the deities, their objective is to spread. This one seems to be able to predict or at least appear to predict human intentionality. We can't let it catch up with the fact that we are destroying its hosts, it will only increase its efforts to evade containment."

"Plus," said another, "the couple of people who did get to more advanced stages . . ." she hissed through her teeth, "It changed their thinking. They did not know who they were."

"We should at least tell their families that we're not trying to save them. Let them say goodbye." Rhododendron.

"We can't." Vard.

"Think of them as soldiers, not patients. What we have done is an act of resistance against an invading enemy," added the tattooed tech. "But they would die either way. It's medically induced coma or internal hemorrhaging, dying in slow pain. I know which I'd choose."

"What I don't understand," began Vard, "is why what happened to Juniper was so . . ." He pursed his lips.

"Explosive." Ella furnished.

The tech's phantom nodded enthusiastically while Ming stepped into him to read the plate he was holding. "The deity did have a completely different effect on her, may she rest in peace.

"This physical symptom, it's bone. Brittle osteophytes growing out of the victim's own skeleton. It seems to be a reaction to a huge acidic imbalance in the victim's blood—which we guessed from the black coloring you can see in the bone itself. Of course, we do not know how the deity achieves this nor can we find out or we risk infecting ourselves."

"We need our damned deimancers," Vard.

"Yes, that's another thing," said the tech. "Juniper and the deimancers it killed immediately. With these people it just doesn't seem interested. The ones without the visions especially. They're dying casually, for want of a better word."

Avon frowned, looked to Vard briefly before saying, "That sounds a hell of a lot like a controlled assassination. A coordinated attack. These poor people are . . . incidents from loose shrapnel."

"I hope so." said Rhododendron, and Speaker's ghost nodded because Rhododendron had spoken. "That would mean it isn't spreading farther."

The three members of the Military faction shook their heads in concern but waited for the tech to explain.

"If," he began, "and it's a big 'if,' that was a planned, coordinated attack, then this deity can identify individuals."

Rhododendron said, "Meaning?"

"No no," the other tech took over, to the first's annoyance. "We know that it can see something that we can temporarily call *intention*. That's why it gives the impression—we think—of being able to glimpse the future. It can reasonably guess what the world, of which human beings are a part, is going to do. Its destruction of the deimancer ring makes perfect sense. Pure self-preservation."

"But Juniper?" Vard.

"I do not believe that it would have identified her as a particular threat," Avon said. "She was an architect."

"Blew her right up though, didn't it?" Ella.

"Yeah." The tattooed tech zoomed into a corner of his plate. "We got everyone who was near Her Highness when it happened to re-create their position in the room." The plate projected upward, showing them a rectangular grid with a cross at its center and human figures arranged around it. "The cross represents Juniper, and then I've highlighted everybody who was infected in red. They're all accounted for." Ming and Xar crowded around the tech, the ghostly emperors joining them. "I've also pinpointed exactly where on their bodies the osteophytes first grew. Look."

"Oh, that's creepy." Ella.

"It is, isn't it?" said the tech.

"What the hell does it mean?" Avon placed her finger on the cross of Juniper's demise and from there began to trace through the highlighted points. They were clearly entry and exit wounds. Moving in a straight line but changing directions in an unpredictable pattern. "This isn't scattered shot from an explosion. Is it a stray bullet ricocheting? No. Look, it goes through three people here before changing direction, only one here. It isn't losing velocity . . . oh yes it is. Look, here and here it stops."

"But it starts again," the tech said. "And we've checked the people between these marks, they're fine. Spotless."

Daksha, "Like it's learning to hide itself. Oh gods. Oh gods what are the implications there? What is it doing?"

"It's looking for someone," whispered Ming. "Xar?"

"Pause the holo," called the Apechi commander. "I don't know. It doesn't look right. But I don't know what right looks like."

"There's no point in us watching the rest of this anyway," sighed Speaker, "we all get swarmed by mites in a few seconds. There's nothing else."

Ming ignored this. "Yes. Yes. We don't know what 'right' looks like. You're only used to seeing the god infecting children. If only the priest were here."

"This thing gets into children?" Speaker.

"On Apech, yes," Kis said thoughtfully. "It tests us all. If it doesn't like you it takes your mind away, leaves you stupid. *Tama* we call them. Doesn't even think they're important enough to kill them. Just rots them away over time."

"They're fun to play with," Ming started. "They can't learn, can't talk. Like walking comas. Makes them amusing."

"*Tama*," repeated Speaker. "It won't . . . it won't do that to me, will it?"

"I'm surprised it hasn't. You are unbearable." Kis.

"There's time yet. But see. It was *looking* for something. See?" Ming.

"It can't be looking for something. I've told you. That's not how deities work." Speaker.

"You keep saying that you don't know how deities work." Kis.

"No, but we have an idea. Several theories." Speaker.

"Which are?" Kis.

Ming fired a warning look at Speaker which the steward did not catch.

"Oh, well some people think that we're living in a computer simulation and deities are glitches, some people think that we're all dead and they're efforts to entertain us by whatever is keeping our souls in purgatory. That kind of thing."

Unusually light of voice, Xar said, "Excuse me?"

"We should put a pin in this." Ming.

"No, no we should not. I don't trust your pins, you're always pinning."

"Don't get overexcited."

Speaker's eyes flicked between the two of them with growing interest.

"Overexcited? Why should I be overexcited? We're all *dead*?"

"We're not dead, Xar."

Fascinated that Xar Kis seemed to be afraid of something which to themself seemed so commonplace Speaker said, "Well, we might be."

"We might be!?"

"Shh," Ming hissed, "there are people watching us and you are being unstable. We will talk about this later. It doesn't matter anyway."

"What do you mean it doesn't—Wait You've said this before, that you don't think we're real. I thought you were just being sinister. Did you know? You knew! You knew this whole time! You've been letting me walk around not being real!"

"Well we're definitely real." Speaker. "Did Adora Ming tell you we aren't real? That seems maternally irresponsible."

"Don't you talk about my mother. Listen. We cannot argue in public."

"OK. Everybody out. Leave us. Now." This was Speaker's voice, loud, a command. They seemed as surprised as anyone that all the techs obeyed. Quieter they continued, "Ming's right. It really doesn't matter."

"How can it not matter? What are you both, what is this place?"

Ming reached her black-gloved hand out to Xar's face. He caught it, she flinched. Speaker saw her eyes begin to water above her mask, which frightened the steward more than anything Xar had ever done before.

"Xar," she hissed, "let go."

He did.

"You will have to speak to the techs, not us," Speaker said. "We don't know about this stuff."

"How can you not know? How can you not care? You govern the world and you don't know what it's made of."

"But that's why we don't care," Speaker soothed. "It doesn't matter, from a political perspective, what we are. It only matters that we are."

"If it doesn't matter then why do you hide it?" Kis complained. "People don't know about this. I didn't know about this."

"There is no 'this' to know. We have no idea what's wrong with the world, just that something *is* wrong with the world." Ming made a movement as if to reach out to him again, changed her mind. "It would only cause panic for people to know that, make them harder to govern. We can't have a universe full of nihilists."

"What do you mean 'something is wrong'?"

"It's the people." Speaker began to explain. "Human beings everywhere. Water everywhere. Liveable planets. It makes no sense, from an evolutionary perspective.

"It could be that the universe itself is alive, of course, that all these planets haven't developed water and air and human beings individually but that the entire thing is evolving together. Or devolving together. Imagine, the entire world not as space containing separate entities but as a uniform creature. A whole body of which we are just a part. So, us running into other humans entire solar systems away is only as puzzling as, I don't know, a blood cell from your ear coming across one from your toe. Is that how that works? And then the deities can be thought of as antibiotics, vitamins even. Designed things that were injected from elsewhere. Who knows. In any case it really, really doesn't matter."

"It matters *to me*."

Cradling her hand Ming said, "What for? It's all just here. We know the deities aren't right. You can feel it, Xar. It's in your body. You know it's not supposed to be here, either that or we aren't. We've known it since the dawn of humanity. We knew it when we were scratching runes into caves to ward off spirits and we know it now when the mathematics doesn't work. There's something wrong, that's all there is to it."

"There's one idea floating around that the world was designed as a simulation, to test out particular environments and circumstances so that the designers could better manage their own societies." Speaker grinned. "That one actually came from an Earth-era sci-fi novel. But according to the people who believe it, the simulation has been abandoned. Running too long and getting buggy. The deities are glitches or, viruses which need to be destroyed before they ruin the whole programming. They think that's what caused the disaster on Earth. It's also why we search for and destroy them, just in case it's true. *We must liberate humanity from the shackles of theism wherever we find them.*" Speaker quoted a Red motto. "You know?"

"You don't have to believe all that. And even if you do, it doesn't change a thing."

"I need a drink." Xar.

Speaker cocked their head at Ming before saying, "Do you mean that?"

"Mean what?" she answered.

"If it's true. If this Apechi deity really is a universe-devouring flaw, you would still pursue rather than destroy it? You would risk eliminating the known world for the sake of a few unnatural powers?"

"I would destroy something that never existed if doing so meant that I got to play with it for a while first, yes. Get the techs back in."

11

"I want a pattern with lines on like yours were. Red and, I like this blue." Back in the grime of Speaker's bathroom, Xar held up a bottle of nail gel.

"You can't have red and blue, that's ridiculous. How about red and pink?" Speaker.

Ming watched her reflection in the broken mirror. Loose skin oozed painlessly beneath the pressure of her thumb as she explored her jaw. Getting out of these rooms had returned to her some sense of direction. She felt like she was winning again. Xar was irritating but the holo had been a confirmation for her. She was right in her conviction that the god was doing something intentional, that they should be following it. She didn't care what anyone else said; it had an idea. It had spoken. It was looking for something. And she was going to find out what.

"I want the blue," Xar complained. "How about black and blue?"

"Could work." Speaker, skeptically. "There should be some black in the bottom of that drawer you're in now."

In the drawer, a piece of paper felt the pressure of Apechi fingers and increasing it, Xar said, "What's this?"

"Nothing. Just a note, I kept it because it's Clara's handwriting."

"Speaker," began Xar, his voice shifted into the elevated tone everybody uses to indicate that they are reading aloud, "I'm about to get catastrophically high. I'm going to be so high by the time you get back that I cannot talk. I am going to be so high that I cannot think. Might have some stupid film on in the background, but it won't be anywhere near as stupid as I. However, right now I am completely sober and with full knowledge of the consequences I want you to know that there is nothing I do not enthusiastically consent to. Like literally nothing. I am going to be so wet for you, that is all I will know. Literally. No thoughts other than wanting you to fuck me. Love you, your girl."

Ming laughed in one humorless breath then asked, "Where is it?"

Knowing what she meant, Speaker answered, "What do you mean?"

"The expiate of course. Where did she keep it? Xar, you'll love this."

"You like expiate?" Speaker.

"What is expiate?" Xar.

Speaker pointed at the note. "I think she described it pretty well. A drug that makes you stupid and, well, you know."

"Wet?" offered Xar, trying to remain calm. "Where is it?"

"If there's any here it's over in those cabinets." Speaker licked their lips. "*You* like expiate?"

"Love it." Ming, already on her way to the guilty cabinets. "I can't believe you've had expiate here this whole time."

Speaker and Xar shared a certain glance.

"Top left," added Speaker.

Xar's eye fell back to the letter. "This makes it sound like she actually wanted to fuck you."

"Wh—what? Of course she did."

The eye accused its way back to Speaker's face. "But you are the most sexless person I have ever met."

"I am *not*."

"Are."

"Got it." Ming turned around, delighted, a vial of pink liquid in one hand.

"I am not sexless."

"Please. We've been talking about the relentless tedium of your relentless life for ages now and not once have you indicated the presence of anything interesting in your—what are you doing?" Kis held his hand up to stop Ming, who was standing over him with a pipette full of the thick, syrupy drug in her unbound hand.

"Open your mouth," she commanded.

"You want *me* to drink that?" he responded. "I thought you were going to. I'm not drinking that. Get away from me."

"I am not sexless. I've written sex scenes. I'll read you a sex scene."

"Open your mouth," Ming demanded.

"I absolutely will not," Xar replied, then stuck out his tongue for the dropper.

"Found one. I'll read it. Listen. Are you listening?"

Clara walked in from the gym. She was still panting, flushed and drenched with sweat. I watched her drink, so greedy for water that the volume she drank distended her wet, muscular stomach. She watched me watching her. Shower with me, she said, and I told her I wasn't dirty. She grinned with half of her mouth, the other spilling water, scooped up the dripping moisture from between her breasts and flicked it at me. You are now, she said, and my eyes stung. I wanted more and I showed her that I did, kneeling, tugging down her tight damp shorts and fixing my mouth to the crease of her cunt while she worked the rest of the sweat down toward my waiting tongue. Tastes like body and filth. I pawed at her shoes and understanding me she shook them off, stumbled, I swung her around mid-movement so she fell back onto our clean white sheets. She laughed but I didn't want to hear it. I balled up the shorts in my hand so they'd keep her knees together as I pushed them up to her shoulders, ass and feet in the air. I spat the sweat I hadn't swallowed onto her exposed little cunt and bit the arches of her feet. She hated that. She squirmed but didn't complain so I stuffed the shorts between her knees into her mouth so she would stay quiet and hold herself in that position for me. She was such a good girl. I went for her ass with my tongue and just about drowned in the well of grease and slime between her fat pussy lips. What? What? What's funny?

"I just didn't know you had it in you. I've never heard you talk like this. I'm actually entertained, if only by how predictably unerotic you make everything sound." Xar's words were beginning to slur. Turning to Ming he said, "Why don't you go the gym?"

Ming raised an eyebrow in the eldritch monstrosity of her face and repeated, "The gym."

Kis groped at the clasp at the front of her robe and said to Speaker, "Go on."

"You're not going to—to fuck about it are you?"

"Of course we are."

The Zetland's occupiers laughed, and Speaker laughed with them.

12

Scales fluttered around the barbs of its skin, shimmering in a placid tide of air. The creature banked to the left. Injured, tired, lost. Its body twisted and its eyelids drooped as the hallway's airflow relieved its muscles some effort. The red fan of its tail pulsed, furling and unfurling with a self-soothing ripple of scarlet hide. Its beak went onomatopoeia sharp clack-clack-clack. The animal part of its brain relaxed, a little. Perhaps it could sleep. Perhaps it could wake somewhere else.

Something in the rhythms of the air changed its mind.

The scales flattened, streamlining against the body, coiling a helix to defend itself. Too exhausted to flee anymore. It could hear them.

Awakening, ink pouring over paper, the creature's divine parasite stirred. The body teemed with a spectral sentience, feeling out the human beings just beyond its vision, craving them. It could bargain with these attackers—give them the power to swim air and take from them some space. It was afraid of them but it knew that it could use them to heal, to grow back into what it once was.

At the end of the hallway, Xar Kis placed his hand on the shoulder of a Crysthian captain. He asked, "Does it know that we're here?"

The captain nodded, turned to look at the usurper. "See."

Already squatting, Xar lowered his face to the floor to catch the god-thing's reflection in the mirror she held.

"It *looks* like we could take it out with guns," whispered another, crouching behind them. The deities that crawled the Zetland were weak and dying, but they were still unpredictable.

Kis nodded. "Yes. But we've been surprised before. I don't want to risk it just yet. I don't like the way this one moves."

"I can feel it, can you?" said the captain. Her subordinates nodded.

The Apechi commander said, "Don't let it tempt you, keep your feet on the ground."

"What's it feel like?" whispered an Apechi soldier, tapping a Crysthian with his knife. The Crysthian did not react like this was an insult.

"Like . . ." the soldier squinted, "I'm being shown parts of the air that could carry my weight. Gentle pulls."

Already sacrosanct, devotees of a different god, the Apechi soldiers were not vulnerable to the possessing godmagic which these creatures could wield. They could not feel offerings, metaphysical bargains, but the Crysthians could.

"Hmm," mused Kis, "strong then, this one. Leave it with us, I don't want any of your team to start floating."

The Military captain disagreed. "Let's just throw a few hits at it, see if anything lands, and then run. We can come back later knowing for certain how to, or at least how not to, do damage."

The captain was young and clever, one of the first to switch allegiances from Ella to Kis when the godthings overwhelmed the Zetland. Her pragmatism saved her cohort and elevated her rank. There were others like her, so many in fact that they vastly outnumbered the loyalist remnants now sealed within the Military wing.

"Captain," whispered one of the Apechi, "where's it gone?"

Her chin shot back to the corner, she tilted the mirror. Right there. Beak black and sharp like filed stone and the power of a spring behind it. Her jaw dropped, her breath caught. The others understood her face, readied their weapons.

Kis's finger to his lips, his other hand closed around a railway spike.

The creature came for them. It was lighter than it should have been, but what made it lighter also made it faster. Its scales were rough, its barbs burned. Its body flashed like a red ribbon, leaving pieces of itself on the skin where it hit—even through dermal armor. It was no longer an animal with an animal brain but a haunted flesh and so the loosened scales had the sense to burrow into the soldiers' bodies when detached. Static electricity cracked as it glided, so delicate that the air's friction burst into little blue stars.

"Fins!" yelled Xar Kis, "Hit the fins!"

Soldiers aimed at the rippling fans which were like sails for the sparkling wyrmbody. It was under their combined assault, holes ripped in its mandible oars, barbs torn from its face. It knew that it couldn't continue, it wanted to lie down in the air, it wanted them to leave it to die. But the creature was the puppet, the parasite its master. It pulled into retreat, the god's power desperate to save this last bastion of its existence in the world.

The captain did not see the whip of the creature's tail as it retreated. Kis saw the captain not see it come, threw her down and absorbed the blow in his own, sacred torso. The Apechi divinity roared inside him, screaming away the pain and showing him what was going to happen.

A vision swam before his eyes in an instant. The godthing won't trigger the trap because it flies—but the soldiers pursuing it will. Three of them, two Crysthians and one Apechi, blown to shreds by a Military claymore. The loyalists who set it must have known that this creature was strong and so expected the Apechi commander to come after it himself, without the theo-vulnerable Crysthians by his side.

Xar's god has shown him the future, now he shows his god that he knows how to use it.

"It's injured," he croaks, doubling over and grasping his chest, "don't let it get away."

Zealous, they ran past him, their commander, the man who they have seen saving their captain, and their footsteps light up the hallway.

13

"Oh, gods, I can see rib," groaned Speaker, wincing over a tech's shoulder.

Ming smiled and exhaled a breath of anesthetic. She liked the sound of that.

"Almost finished," said the tech. "But I'm going to need to come check it in a few hours. And then every few hours after that, too." He stood back to admire his work, transparent sheeting over the geometric lines that Ming had carved into her torso.

"Ming?" a man in a Red uniform cleared his throat. "We were saying about the . . . uhh . . . about—"

"About Daksha," snapped Speaker, tossing their glittering hair to reveal earrings and a face carefully dotted with golden paint.

"What about her?" Ming.

"We, um. Our scouts' ship is approaching Wresh. They have it in sight. We should hear back before long. A few days."

"Have you relayed . . ." Her voice was languid from the anesthetic, but her mind still sharp, "Our scouts aren't to alert the ground to their presence, they aren't to move if they find Daksha or her section of the Zetland. They aren't to take their eyes off her."

"Y-yes, ambassador," stammered the man. He did not know whether Speaker or Ming was the highest-ranking Red in the room. He didn't know whose side he was supposed to be on. Or if there were sides at all. He wished someone would tell him.

At that moment the door flew open with a confidence which meant that only Xar could be behind it. He stepped in as it swung, shoulders bowed slightly with the pain of the godthing's assault, saying, "They're practically rioting in the main hall, Ella is absolutely—what the fuck is this?" He stopped in his tracks, taking in the Reds, the tech, Speaker, Ming's mangled face.

Seeming to come alive she sat upright, reached for her mask, fixed it to her ear. She did this with a fumbling haste which told Speaker, for the first time, that she was wearing it at Xar's instruction.

"Everybody get out," Xar purred, and even the tech almost ran from the room. Speaker did not move.

"You're hurt," Ming said. "You shouldn't have sent the tech—"

"Listen. Ella and his fools left a trap for me in the hallways near the library. The trap killed Crysthians." He smiled. "Everyone's very angry about it."

"Excellent." Ming.

"How many are dead?" Speaker.

"Only a couple. One of mine, as well. But . . . it has really stirred something this time."

Ming's fingernail rattled across the ridges of her mask before she said, "They are sick of being reminded that their world has changed."

"They are 'sick' of death and fear," said Speaker.

"Whatever."

"The point is," continued Xar, "that I think some of the Crysthian teams might be ready to help me with Ella. It will demoralize his base to see it."

Ming hissed through her teeth in an "I don't know about that" way.

Speaker said, "I thought you needed him alive."

"Yes . . ." said Kis, turning to look at the steward, "the prophet told us to bring him to her. But what has that got to do with using Crysthians against him?"

Speaker shrugged. "If my own people started attacking me, I'd just kill myself."

"That's because you're a pussy."

"No, Speaker has a point." She sighed. "Everything's so fucking boring all the time."

Xar poked thoughtfully at the new contraption around Ming's torso. "I like that I can see your insides. But really, this thing with the dead soldiers, we should use this. We can slip into a firmer place of command."

"Yes." Ming closed her hand possessively around his. "I will speak to the captains, as commander."

How dare you, Speaker almost said, but then the god of Apech told them not to.

It was the first time Speaker had experienced a true vision since Clara's death. It begins with déjà vu.

It can be like a dream, it can play out in real time or it can be a second. You can see it clearly or it can just be a feeling. A feeling of irrevocable truth.

The insult left Speaker's lips, and Xar's hand was at their throat. Ming screams for him to stop, leaping after him and pulling desperately at his sanctified arms not to break the steward but he was already so angry and he can't help himself. He hooks his thumb around Speaker's throat and it will crack it will go right through—

It was over.

Speaker gasped, sweating and wide-eyed. They looked to Kis, who was staring back, the god rippling its attention over his face.

"Confess." Xar.

"Wh . . . what?"

"Confess. What did it just show you?"

Ming sat upright. "What's this?"

"Speaker just saw something. A vision. I can see it too, evidence of it I mean, I don't know what it was."

Speaker stuttered.

"What was it?" Ming's voice turned urgent, desperate. "The god showed you something? What did it say? What does it want?"

"I—I—It showed me." Still gasping. The vision had hurt, Speaker had felt the terror and the certainty of death. "It showed me that Xar would kill me, if I insulted you."

"Which means," Xar began toward Speaker, who stood and backed away, hands raised, "that you were going to."

"Xar, stop it. It doesn't matter. Stop." He obeyed her voice. "This is huge. This is the first time it's visited you since Clara?"

Speaker nodded.

"I knew it! I knew it!" she shrieked, her fists clenched in triumph. "I told you!"

Xar frowned but said nothing.

"Knew what?" Speaker.

"First Clara and now this? Think about it, for fuck's sake. It's keeping you alive! It's doing it on purpose! It *was* looking for you. See! I'm right. I'm fucking right!"

"But the prophet says—"

"Fuck the prophet!"

"*The prophet says* that deities don't behave like that. With that kind of intentionality, not unless someone's controlling them." Xar, being reasonable.

Ming made enraged dismissive gestures, arms everywhere, while Speaker said, "You—hang on, you don't know?"

"Know what?" Xar asked.

"That it *meant* to infect me. I thought you at least knew that, although now I'm realizing I don't know why I thought that. This whole time, you haven't known?"

"Not for sure, not for sure, but we do now!" Ming said.

"Ming." Xar began to laugh. "We don't know anything. We weren't even sure it was a deity at first. We don't even know what it's a deity of."

Ming scowled. "We're getting there."

"What it's . . . of?" Speaker. "What do you mean?"

"You know," Xar, lightly. "God of. God of war, god of windowsills, god of wastewater. We don't have a clue."

Speaker stared. "Are you joking? That's not even . . . that's not even how you're supposed to think about deities they aren't *of* something. They're unnatural. Tell me you're joking."

"Nope." Xar was still laughing, Ming was not.

Speaker raised their hands in a new disbelief, a new dread. It was amazing to them that there could still be new dreads at that point. "You . . . you . . . You've used a deity which you don't understand *at all* to overthrow us? You've let it get everywhere and you don't have the faintest idea *what it is*?"

"Yes!"

Voice cracking like she was laughing beneath the mask, Ming said, "We did do that, didn't we?"

"Oh my fucking gods! What are we going to do! What the fuck! Why would you allow this!"

Ming shrugged.

"Wait, wait," Xar laughed, "it gets better. There was this one man who knew what it was, how to control it. He did all this horrible, weird taxidermy. Embarrassing. Rude man, didn't like him at all."

"And it fucking *ate* him." Ming.

"It *ate* him?! What do you mean? What the fuck? You people are insane! It ate him?!"

"Ate the fuck out of him. He was its last—its only—priest and it chewed his bones. No idea why." Ming sat down. "Oh fuck. Oh, fuck."

"What do you mean! Why was there only one priest!"

"He was evil," said Xar. "Real horrible evil going on with him."

"They"—Ming flicked her hand at Xar to show she meant Apechi—"were pretending the god didn't exist. They killed all the priests and were trying to act normal so we'd let them into Crysth. They missed one."

"To be clear, you're telling me you're more scared of this priest than an actual errant deity? He's . . . real horrible evil?" Speaker.

"No, he's eaten." Ming.

Xar patted Ming's shoulder. "We'll figure it all out. The prophet knows what to do."

"It eats people." Speaker, tragically. "Perverse."

"Yes but only when it . . ." Xar drew a vague figure in the air with a flutter of both hands, "Manifests. And we don't know how to make it do that."

"Oh there's a relief. I suppose that means you also don't know how to make it not do that, too?"

"Suppose so." Xar, cheerfully.

"It's in our ships. It's in the trains. It's in the fucking *doors*. It has control over everything. It manifests and eats people."

"Yes, yes, whatever. Look, seriously, it has a plan. It isn't random." Ming's voice quickening with excitement. "We know that for certain now. We just need to figure out what its plan actually is."

"So . . . this isn't just about getting it to infect you, it's about getting control of . . . everything. You think that there might be something about me which . . . shows its motives?"

"Correct." Xar.

"But the prophet knows how to talk to it, right?"

"Yes." Ming said. She and Xar shot each other a quick look which, having had enough of existential horror, Speaker decided not to notice. "But she wants Ella first."

"I don't trust her. It's all been too easy. She doesn't seem as if things with her should be easy," commented Xar. "I do like her though."

"She's excellent at behaving like a cult leader is all. The act wouldn't be half as good if she gave the impression of predictability." Ming.

"She *is* a cult leader." Speaker.

"That doesn't diminish how remarkable it is that she knows how to act like one. Now, write down everything you saw in that vision, while it's fresh in your mind. And then retell me about the first time."

"I'm not listening to that again." Xar. "I'm off to sow discord."

"Yes, yes. Speaker, get a pen."

14

I knew I was infected. I knew because I wasn't worried. There's a sort of, you know, a difference between anxiety and doom.

It started in my mouth. I couldn't stop licking it, desperate for it to be some sort of weirdly developed tooth or cancerous growth but too afraid to get it scanned. I suppose all that advance worrying is part of why I came to acceptance so quickly when I finally saw it in the mirror.

The pattern was nothing like the one Xar has. You can see my scars still, even though they're not as deep as his either. His look organic and mine straight, perfectly level. Just regularly spaced spikes poking out of my skin. I could see it in my face, too. It doesn't happen so much anymore, but I can see waves. I see it on Xar all the time; it pays attention to him a lot. It ripples over his body, makes it look like he's in lots of different places at once, lots of different species at once even. I can tell when it's tuning him, showing him things, leading him around. But it mostly leaves me alone.

I was wearing a silk dressing gown. Had to get rid of it after of course but it was very lovely. Tassels, a little fur around the cuffs and neck. I had it open at the front, standing just over there and poking at the bone in my chest. The vision started when I heard the door.

No it didn't. I heard the door in the vision. It was strange. Of course it was strange. But she must have been right behind me the whole time and

I never saw her reflection. Did the god do that, do you think? It added to the fear, when the vision ended and she was suddenly so close.

I had that sense of déjà vu. Overwhelmingly. My head swam, I wanted to sit down but it must have wanted me to stay standing because I couldn't move. I saw her come into the room. I saw her see the spikes. She made eye contact with me and I could see in her face that she was going to tell. I saw deodands dragging me to the medical wing, I saw myself hooked up to those machines that would make me forget that they were killing me. I saw Clara compulsively checking herself, afraid she had caught it from me. I saw the mirror break, and I saw the shard that I would finish her with.

When it was over, the vision I mean, I had this sense of clarity and purpose. The path was unwavering. Like I was possessed. I think I was possessed. Well obviously, I was possessed. I never would have done it. But I saw her suddenly behind me in the mirror, staring at the spikes in the glass. I grabbed her hair and I smashed her into the mirror. She didn't start screaming until it broke. I saw the shard. It was the same one from the vision, the exact same shape and size. So I knew that what I was doing was right. I hated the way she sounded while she choked on it. I had to leave so I couldn't hear.

That's what hurts me the most. I had to kill her, but I didn't stay. I left her to drown in blood and glass, alone on my bathroom floor. It took so long. She didn't deserve to die alone. She didn't deserve to die being held by someone like me, either. She should have been with Rhododendron instead. I bet she would have gone to die with him when I couldn't—not like anybody ever wants to die with me anyway.

It was only afterward, when I knew she was gone, that I realized my seeking knife was right beside me. I could have ended her suffering but I sat and cried instead. Got blood all over my sheets. I think I loved her.

Rhododendron and Haja came. I don't know why. I just summoned the nearest deodand but they went to get him when they saw what was going on. It was awful.

An accident, he kept saying, an accident. Jeering inches away from my face while I sobbed. How can this have been an accident, he said, and I told him that I didn't know.

The deodands were thrilled of course. You'd have to be, to be the type of person selected for their job. They think it's fucking hilarious, or, no they think it's gratifying when we're caught out. They love that everyone in the empire knows that they clean up after us, they love it when we give them something horrible to do.

Anyway I said to him, "It was an accident. I swear to you, as my emperor and my brother, that this was an accident." Gods I'm disgusting.

"This," he spat back at me, "is not accidental. This," he pointed at her body, "is bourgeois!"

I gasped. He stormed off with Haja behind him, leaving me there to watch Clara being cleaned away.

Do you want me to keep going?

Okay.

I don't know how long it was before Rhododendron came back. It felt like an eternity but it can't have been, because he spoke like he was picking up the same thought. Maybe he was ranting about me to Haja the entire time he was out of the room and worked himself into a frenzy.

He was all lit up when he came out with the accusation. Like a giant, patchy firefly. He had so much of his gear on that I could hear it.

"You killed Cull, didn't you?" is what he said.

I couldn't believe it. I was so stunned that it must have looked like my shock was fake, theatrical.

"Why would you think that?" is what I said back.

His eyes narrowed. He looked at me like I was a stranger. "I know you were attracted to him. Don't. Don't contradict me. I hear your heartbeat. I feel your pupils dilate. I track which direction you're looking. I would tune it out if I could, you think I care? But I know. And now I know what you do to your . . . lovers."

"This was an accident.," I said. "I don't know how this happened."

He said, "You know what's fucking appalling, Speaker? I can tell that you think you're telling the truth. Haja."

"She helped you carry Cull's body back to the ship. Did she know what you had done? Did she see you."

"Cull hanged himself."

"Did you make him do it?" she asked.

"How?" I sort of wailed that, but seriously how are you supposed to make a grown man just up and hang himself? A teenager maybe, but not an adult.

"Did you fuck?" Rhododendron asked.

I said that we did not, and then I realized the implications of the question and started shrieking.

What do you mean "Why"? My own brother suggested that having sex with me might drive a man to suicide. Perverse. No it is not funny, it is perverse.

"Look," is what he said eventually, "I know you're not lying but I also don't believe you. It doesn't matter." And then I could tell that he needed to say something he didn't want to because he smiled for her to do it instead.

"This new development could be useful."

I asked what new development she meant and Rhododendron clarified that she meant my "killing spree." I told him I was not on a killing spree, so he told me to shut up.

"With Vard incapacitated . . . " began Haja, "There could be some issues."

I tried to stop sobbing and say "what," then I pointed out that Clara was dead and I was very upset and they were trying to talk to me about politics.

"We don't have time for theatrics, Speaker," Rhododendron said. Which I think was very cruel and unkind of him on reflection. "Knock that off and think. Vard is . . . ill. . . . He cannot appear in public. Ella is his steward."

I stopped sniffling and said, "Oh dear."

"Indeed," agreed Haja. "He's going to try for the throne."

"We cannot have that man in charge of Military. Especially with this new friction between him and Avon. We need unity."

"No, no you're right," I said. "But what's it got . . . " and that's when I realized, you know, what they were saying. So I said, "No!"

"Speaker," said Haja, as if warning a naughty child that she was about to lose her patience. I hate that. I outrank her, you know. "We've already agreed that the two of you will be the ones representing us down there on Wresh. Just . . . make something happen."

Then Rhododendron said, "Make yourself *useful.*"

So I said, "I *am* useful."

I'm useful, aren't I?

I was useful when we were making the decision to head for Wresh. I've never seen the pentagon like that before. Nobody knew who was in charge. Ella was hysterical, Avon was evil, Vard was off being dead. Total nightmare.

The Ethicists were all unruly, too. They must have known that something was seriously wrong with Vard. I don't know how much Daksha told them, but there was never a moment when it wasn't on her face. We'd made up some crap about the library being closed and decided that Vard was in his apartments having an organ transplant, but I bet the only reason anyone believed it is because they wanted to.

Plus, she was obsessed with Jim. Wouldn't let him out of her sight. He was in the pentagon even, standing there with the Ethicists. I suppose she was afraid that if he stopped concentrating or something that Vard might, I don't know, double die.

Even Adora Ming and Haja were being nuts. It was the damned mites on top of everything else, they were painful and annoying and everywhere. Everything fucking sucked.

"No more running," is what Daksha was saying. "No more looking for help. We've already done that. We went to Hecubah so that we could *fight.*"

The real problem was . . . well. There were fucking loads of real problems. But a massive one was that Avon Stal was saying that Vard had agreed to her plan when they'd discussed it privately, and the rest of us had no way of challenging her on this without openly admitting that we didn't know if it was true and couldn't check with Vard because he was dead. Real dilemma.

"Your Highness Daksha," Avon was saying back, standing at the front of the Military cohort on the lowest platform behind Ella, "it will not work. It simply will not work."

"And why not, darling?" is what Ella said, turning around to face her with a little arm flourish that he does when he thinks he's winning.

Avon smiled—I fucking despise that woman—before saying: "You know why."

"Ella." Rhododendron was doing his reasonable voice. "We know that this Apechi deity is not physically located on Apech."

"Do we, though?" retorted one of the Green crowd.

"Yes!" Avon growled. "I fight these things all the time. For almost a century I have been fighting while you . . . draw houses or whatever it is you do. It has been *here*. It is not contained in one physical location . It is metaphysical!"

"Ella told me just a few days ago that he'd defeated a deity in a *sword fight* and you're telling me now that we can't destroy this one with an entire nuclear bomb?" Daksha asked, exasperated.

"Yeah!" said Ella, to the agreement of some of the Military cohort who I assume were more loyal to him than to Avon. "We have been attacked! We need to get them bombed!"

That got a lot of cheers, which I found quite distasteful.

Adora Ming shouted: "That planet is *tiny*. We should destroy the damn thing on principle whether it would completely eliminate the problem or not!"

That got a lot of agreement from Military and oh my gods, Ming, I've just realized—it's because she thought *you* were dead. Was completely out of character for her to interrupt like that but she thought that her daughter had been killed on Apech, didn't she? I wonder what it was like for her when she realized that you were alive, but that you were running the invasion. Does that not make you feel anything? Perverse.

"We don't have time for that shit," snapped Avon. "I know everyone is angry. I know everyone is afraid and that everyone wants to act. But I promise to you all that a bomb would only waste time. The thing is spreading. We need an ally who can fight it on its own terms and Vard agreed—agrees—with me! There is no debate here."

Daksha just stammered in rage, the words seemed not even Crysthian. She was using some outer language with lots of sharp sounds, must have been her native. I can't imagine how angry she must have been. Knowing or, at least suspecting that words were being put into her dead lover's mouth and being unable to say so.

It was Ella who had the idea. It was . . . terrible of him in the moment but it was honestly pretty inspired. Plus I loved to see the look on Avon's face.

Ella said: "No he doesn't."

Avon whispered, "What?"

"I was there." Ella lied, arms up again, "When you were explaining the plan to Vard in his suite. Remember? Vard doesn't agree. He thinks we should all vote on it. I can go ask him again if you like."

I put my hand over my mouth and stared at the back of Rhododendron's head, waiting for him to do something. I think he was doing the same but looking at Avon, waiting for her to do something. Anyway that's when things got really good. Avon stepped up onto the stewards' platform. Yes, she did. On my brother's grave she did. She stepped right up onto there. So she and Ella are standing there facing each other and everybody's dead silent before Avon says, "Alright. Let's vote. With me standing in for Vard."

Ella grinned. "Alright," he repeated, "let's vote. Why don't you do the honor of telling *everyone* exactly where it is you want to go?"

Of course it was over, then. There's no way to retract a statement like that. Once you've floated the idea of knowledge around, you just can't withdraw it. Especially not when everyone's already so rioty.

"We agree. If Avon Stal is proposing that we should vote on something without knowing what it is, then she is proposing a popularity contest," said one of the Greens.

"I am not proposing we should vote on anything. We should be operating under martial law right now. It is irrelevant what the rest of you think."

"Ah! Aha! She admits it!" squawked Ella.

"Of course I admit it, you whinnying moron," is what she said. And I remember that's exactly what she said because who could forget "whinnying moron"? "This is a war! A war that I am in the best position to fight! Have you all forgotten why Vard wanted to come to me in the first place?" Which was a fair point. She's still evil though.

"Seeking your counsel is not a guarantee of its acceptance," said one Green or the other.

Daksha nodded. "I also believe that the . . . very extreme nature of the general's proposition demands its full disclosure. Rho?"

"Yes, you're right. Avon, we should tell them."

Ella smiled at her, as he had been doing the whole time, then repeated: "Tell them where you want to go."

She bowed ironically then flipped over her right arm to show the demonstration which she'd done for the rest of us already.

Yes, I know this part is important. Threatening me isn't going to make me remember it any more clearly.

"Our enemy, as we all know, is what we call a deity." She started walking around the room so that everybody could see the holos illustrating her words. Not that they were needed. "People tend to imagine deities as ghosts or specters which can possess single, corporeal hosts. From there, they can contaminate and spread into human beings and, as we have recently discovered, the low-grade sentiences which we use to power most of our technology.

"This understanding, of a single focal point which can be destroyed and destroy the deity itself, is sometimes correct. This one however spreads without contact or proximity to a central manifestation. Our best guess is that it is able to contaminate anywhere, or anyone, of whom it is somehow aware. We believe that it uses a host's memory to create predictions about our behavior. This would explain how it has managed to so thoroughly contaminate our machines. The demons are a network, they whisper to each other constantly. It gets into one, it gets into them all.

"So we cannot think of the Apechi deity as a block, but more as a ripple. A wave flowing back and forth with multiple sources of influence. We can destroy sources of influence but it will only create more. It is everywhere. It's shocking we're all alive. We can only assume that the Apechi priests or deimancers, whatever they call those who understand it, are interested in control rather than destruction. They want to take over our empire, not annihilate it."

Of course now I know that you insane people don't have deimancers or priests and it's just running around doing whatever the fuck. I know you think it has a plan but it can't have a plan. Okay, okay.

Ella interrupted at that point and said, "So we should assassinate the people who are controlling it. And we can reasonably guess that they are on Apech!"

"Even if," Avon held up her hands to ward off the catastrophe of noise that Ella's outburst had caused, "the priests of Apech are all on Apech, killing them would mean that the deity is left to its own devices. Imagine that. A completely unpredictable, unnatural force, in charge of Crysth. A god on the throne. Something without mind or intention or rationality being in complete control of what we have built. That is what I am talking about here." Yes. Imagine that.

"Oh," said one of the Greens, which captured the general mood.

Avon raised a welcoming palm to Rhododendron. He said, "Comrades, this is why I believe we should accept the general's proposition. Even if we shatter all known physical locations of this deity, which because of the extent of the demon-grid would mean technological paralysis for *decades*, that is no guarantee that it would be gone from the ether. We have no method within the empire which is capable of locating this deity on its own level."

"So . . ." said a Green, "the suggestion is that we go beyond the empire for help?"

Avon nodded. It was tense. Those of us at the very top knew what was coming and we were bracing ourselves for everybody's reaction. They could feel our anxiety.

"You're saying that we have built rigid structures on unstable terrain," said a Green. "You're saying we need to visit an architect who knows how to design an earthquake-proof structure." She looked up at the largest of the holo ripples, bouncing back and forth across the room. "An expert in tsunami-resistance."

Avon grinned at her. "Yes! Well, almost. I'm saying that we need someone who knows how to *surf* the tsunami."

"Tell them who you mean," said Daksha. "Enough of this. Just say it."

I could tell that a few of the black hands had already worked it out. I could hear them whispering.

"I would seek the help of the Ma empire's prophet, U6-93."

So that was pandemonium.

Daksha was gratified, standing there with her knuckles on the table while everyone roared around the edges of the room.

Rhododendron allowed for around thirty seconds of cacophony before he stood too. Now that shut everybody up pretty quickly because he never uses his height. He was always a bit of a skulker.

"A theocrat, Rhododendron, and you're about to defend this?" yelled Ella.

"Please remain calm," is what my brother replied. "The Ma empire has never expressed any violence toward Crysth for its own sake."

"Darling that's only because they're too busy acting like spacefreaks! They're evil!"

"Your tone, Ella," repeated Rhododendron, so Ella did a "oh sorry Your Highness" in a big fluff of air. Then Rhododendron said something like, "I will choose to accept that apology for the good of this conversation only. Now, Ma and Crysth are obviously not allies. We have clashed over territorial advancements in the past, granted—"

"Rho," Daksha interrupted. "Respectfully, I do not give a shit about the history of diplomatic relations between our two empires. The fact of the matter is that any allegiance, however temporary, however small, with those people would undermine the very core of our collective moral and ideological values."

"Your Highness," said Avon Stal, "I propose that such an allegiance would undermine our collective moral values much less than would our annihilation. U6-93 is the closest thing in the known world to a true expert on deities. The god of the Ma empire can and will destroy the god of Apech. Please do not forget that it is I who has 'clashed' with her over territorial advancements. I have dealt with her before. I know what she can do."

Daksha's argument was that it wasn't about what the prophet *can* do but what she does do. She expands her territory only to satiate the deity she serves, to entertain it, with no concern for the people that she destroys in the process. It means U6-93 cannot be negotiated with. You should think about that too, you know. I know you think she's helping you but her god is a cannibal. I don't know why you're convinced that it won't consume yours, just like Avon said.

That's all there was of Avon's speech as far as the Apechi deity was concerned. She won the whole "should we see the evil bastards or not" thing by arguing that we would be turning up with a request that U6-93 does something that she wants to do anyway—to set her god loose on another. We'd basically be taking her a slab of meat on a silver platter, plus some other treaties etcetera to sweeten the sweet deal even further. Sounded great at the time. What stupid cunts we all were.

What's important is that after all that had been decided it was *me* who suggested we fumigate the Zetland first. Well, a tech had suggested it in a Red meeting but it was me who suggested it to the Pentagon. Everybody agreed that we would land on Wresh and congratulated me for giving us all something to look forward to. Finally no more mites. So, see? I am useful.

15

When we arrived on Wresh, the hell we were in started to feel like a hell designed specifically for me. I'd been sent on an assassination mission. What was I supposed to do? I had no idea. Clara would have been able to figure something out for me. Oh and I was syphilitic with your horrible Apechi god-curse, which I'll admit was bothering me only vaguely because I had opted to pretend it didn't exist.

It was me who had suggested Wresh. I thought it would be the best possible place to land the Zetland for a few days while it zapped the mites because they don't use our machines and aren't involved in any of our diplomatic issues. We just needed ground space and air. But it meant that I felt responsible for the whole ordeal. Well, I *was* responsible for the whole ordeal, but you know what I mean. There was a moment up in the Red control room when we thought we wouldn't get clearance to land at all, and I found myself hoping that would be the case. Just couldn't bear the thought of the liability.

Wresh has a planetary policy against "alien association"; they never leave, we never go. Perverse, really. It depressed me. They have so much potential and squander it by doing nothing.

The council that finally allowed us to land was located in the northern part of their globe. Beautiful, heavily forested place but unbearably hot and muggy. I had to pack my sleeveless dresses without the proper tunics.

It made me look like someone who listens exclusively to electropop but believes they're doing so ironically. Of course once we got down there I found out that they'd never actually let us leave the building we were staying in, so the unnecessary wardrobe impairment was really getting on my nerves.

It took them, a state called Samfé, less than a day to clear what they described as a "guest tower" for us. Rhododendron and Avon took as many as possible onto her ship and waited in the sky, while the rest of us packed into Samfé like refugees—which we were, but it felt undignified.

Samfé has a spaceport, but it was too small for the palace so we landed basically straddling what I believe must have been a waste treatment plant of sorts. There was barely a hello before we were packed onto a train which took us through an underground lake to a station beneath the tower. It was quite rude.

The train itself was lovely, an aquatic glass carriage to give you a view into the water. Vaguely frightening, utterly stunning. Imagine rays of light shining down into a giant black abyss, multicolored jellyfish flashing like lanterns, larger shadows snaking far below. It's rare that I get to see a view which actually makes me want to look. I was sorry the journey was so brief.

The tower they gave us was less interesting but equally lovely. A spiral with conveyer walkways moving around a waterfall feature encased in glass so it ran silently down the building. They corralled us and watched us like hawks. They also tried to put Ella, Daksha, and I into rooms which were really far apart from each other. We made a little complaint and ended up in a row of four with Jim on the far side; just tiny guest suites like you might find in a hotel back home. Maybe that's what it was.

Anyway like I was saying, the beauty and the technological mastery of it all made me a bit manic. The view from the window was like nothing I've seen in another city. Well it was kind of normal, it just felt different. I can't explain it. Projections into the sky and onto the sides of buildings which seemed to be just gorgeous for the hell of it. Hundreds of single-carriage trains zipping around the place on rails above. Giant watermills turning between all the towers. People flying kites. All that, and they don't leave their planet. It's just such a waste. So damned provincial. What's the point? That's what upset me. I remember thinking, what the hell is the point of you all? Can you imagine waking up every morning knowing that you'll never go anywhere, never do anything beyond the confines of this one, tiny lifetime, this one, tiny planet? Just unbearable.

I was also supposed to be killing Ella. One big thing that held me back was that the spikes in my skin from the Apechi deity hadn't fully receded. If I got killed too then everyone would see them and know that I had hidden the virus, then think that I had killed Ella out of madness rather than because he deserved it. But that's what you get for being me.

But obviously I just kept putting it off. I considered lunging for him a few times in the hallway or at dinner but it was just too ridiculous. He gave me the only real opportunity himself, whispered at me on the walkway to be alone in my room in an hour. That was a bad hour. Waiting there in my electropop dress with blaze of glory intentions and a tiny little seeking knife in my glove. Pathetic.

I had no idea what he wanted and didn't care until he pranced into my room screaming. It's hard not to care about something when it's being screamed into your face. He's charismatic in a vulgar sort of way.

What he was saying was, "Daksha needs an intervention. She's lost her mind. She's trying to kidnap Jim."

So naturally I said something along the lines of, "Pardon me?"

He exclaimed a "darling" at me and then lay on my bed like he couldn't take any more of the world before saying, "Daksha says she's staying here."

That took me by surprise. I stopped looking for parts of him that looked stabbable and started to listen. "What, in Samfé?"

"Of course in Samfé! And they're letting her. She's talking about detaching the Ethicist wing from the Zetland and staying here with Jim!" I asked why and he said, "Because she's out of her mind with grief obviously darling. We need to stop her."

I thought about it for a moment and told him that honestly if Samfé were willing to let her stay then it might not be a bad thing. She wasn't on board with the plan and she obviously was in fact out of her mind with grief. Which anybody would be, considering the circumstances. Let her recover.

He got to his feet at that and started pacing. "Are you mad? You've been floating off somewhere in that weird narrow," and he did say narrow, "head of yours for a while as well. Do you pay no attention? Honestly. I feel like everybody's gone totally mad but me. Everybody!" Of course now I know he was correct but that really sounds like something someone who has gone mad would say, doesn't it?

"What are you actually talking about?"

"These Samfé people," he said, in a way which made "Samfé" sound like a slur. "Are up to something. How have you not noticed?" He waved his arm at the walls and whatnot. "Look!"

There was stuff missing. They had clearly removed screens or controls or something from our rooms. Wondering where I was going to stab him again, I said, "What is the problem?"

"Speaker, you are so mentally boring." Unfair of him, I thought. "They are hiding tech from us. As if we're thieves or . . . idiots. We have our own tech! We don't need their crap."

"You're mad because they don't want us to play with their toys?" I was kind of trying to make him angrier. Be easier to kill him if he kept insulting me.

"No! Because they think their toys are better than ours!"

"That's really stupid."

"Who do they think they are!"

I just shook my head.

He clicked his tongue and sat back on my bed. "Darling. Seriously, what is the matter with you? You know Daksha's gone wrong. She won't leave Skull Shoes alone. She won't do anything. And it's downright weird that these people would allow her to stay. Almost the entire planet rejected us, Rhododendron said, and now suddenly they're happy to indefinitely host part of the Zetland and one of its emperors? Why do they have a spaceport? Who has been visiting them? Why can't we leave this tower? They're hiding something. What's their angle, Speaker? Come on. Help me out here. I feel insane."

"Why don't you just ask them what's missing if it's bothering you so much?"

He gave me a look of total bewilderment. I feel a bit bad about that. I was sort of teasing him wasn't I, missing his point on purpose.

"You're just mad because it's nicer than Crysth," is what I said next.

He gasped, hand over his heart. "How dare!"

"It's true," I said, goading him. "They're out there flying kites."

"That's not nice, that's insufferable!"

"All I'm saying is that Daksha might be due a little relaxation. The Zetland is not a positive psychological environment at this time."

He stood up again, sat back down. Mouth open. I'd almost forgotten the assassination, I was too distracted by the inner ordeal he seemed to be having. He said, "Are you not hearing me? I feel. I feel insane, Speaker. Nobody is hearing me. These people are up to something! This isn't about Daksha needing to recover, this is about these anti-space hermit fuckers being up to something! I feel like . . . everyone's just going along with stuff all the time and stuff keeps going wrong but nobody will stop and listen to me."

That's when he started crying. I didn't know what to do at all. How are you supposed to stab a crying person? It would be totally perverse.

"I'm sorry," he said. "I just . . . everything's a disaster."

"I know." What else was I supposed to say? It was. I went to get him a tissue. Even their tissues down there were better than ours, you know.

I sat next to him and let him cry. I suppose I should have been reassuring him instead of tapping my nails together but I didn't even notice I was doing it until he yelled at me to stop. So at least it bolted him out of his little reverie. Wait not reverie. What's the opposite of a reverie? His little spiritual collapse. Anyway.

"You're right," is what I said after I apologised for the nail tapping. I told him that everything was wrong, everything kept happening too quickly, nobody was properly in charge, and it all felt fucked.

"It isn't usually like this," he answered, "even when it's bad. I know what you all think of me. No, darling, don't do that. I know you all think I'm brash and annoying, but I am a godsforsaken commander of our Military and I have been in some dire situations. It never felt like this. We are charging downhill."

"We just feel lost without Vard and Cull."

"And Juniper. And now we're losing Daksha. And frankly Rhododendron isn't being particularly helpful either."

"You just think that because he's agreeing with Avon Stal."

"Do you agree with her?"

I said that I didn't know.

We became friendly after that. I was unconvinced that Daksha ought to remain with us aboard the Zetland and made that abundantly clear, but I did consent to perform some light espionage in an attempt to calm his nerves. It was on that account that I had perhaps the most depressing conversation of my life. With Jim, obviously. Daksha was stonewalling as she usually does when the Ethicists are scheming, so Ella suggested we try getting information out of the necromancer instead. It was awful. Just getting him on his own was hard enough but the interaction that followed was pure despair.

"This is happily ever after," is what he kept saying. Still through the translator. I wonder if it produced the cliché for him, or if that is truly what he meant. Unbearable either way. "Samfé is welcoming, prosperous, beautiful. There are no dead. There is nobody reading your mind. Nobody to flee, nobody to fight. They are friendly to us. This is happily ever after."

"This is a dead end." I was practically in tears.

He shook his head like he was sad for me. "You are like an adolescent afraid of its parents' domesticity." And what the fuck does that mean? "You think that you need to be unhappy to be alive." Fuck off. All things of a similar nature he said to me. Can you believe such people exist, such mediocrity? What's the point?

I explained that there were two big problems in his plan of nonaction. One, Samfé definitely want something in return and if they're not saying clearly what it is then that's because it's something they know you don't want to give. Two, it is extremely likely that Apech will chase Daksha . . . Xar's here.

*

"Hm? Oh, good." Ming lay in the shade of an oak tree. A brook gurgled over stone. False ruins floated offensively on platforms overhead. There were other people in the gardens too, Apechi and Crysthian. Kept at a distance by Ming's guards, not that they would want to approach.

But Xar carried a storm with him. A hard, tired face. He knelt between them.

"What's wrong?" Ming.

"Daksha is not in Samfé."

Speaker's heart leapt. "What?"

"You heard me. She's not there." His voice dropped to a whisper. "Where has she gone?"

"I have no idea. I thought she was in Samfé. I only asked Jim to convince her to come with us. That's what Ella wanted me to—"

"How can you be sure?" said Ming. "They could be hiding her."

"I said that. But none of the Crysthian techs can think of a way these Samfé people could hide a quarter of the fucking Zetland."

"Respectfully. . . . There was evidence of quite a lot of . . ." Speaker began. "Look, if they have stealth tech that we don't, I would not be surprised."

"We're not just scanning," Kis, still whispering. "Ming made sure we have physical eyes on the place. It's not there."

"They could have dismantled it." Ming, unconvinced by herself.

"What were you going to do, anyway?" Speaker. "Apech can't invade Wresh, there aren't enough of you and they use hydro or solar power or something."

"No, Apech can't invade Wresh. Crysth can though, and we are Crysth." Ming.

"Shit." Speaker.

"Where else could she be, Speaker? Help me think." Xar.

"I have no idea. How could I possibly know? She's the Ethicist emperor, I am—was—the Red steward. Why would I know what she's up to?"

Xar slumped into the picnic blanket. Polka-dot. Ming ignored him, watched Speaker crawl over to pour him a cup of tea. Peppermint. She suppressed a smile. "Are you sure they're telling you the truth? Daksha is an emperor after all. Those we sent to look might not want to find."

"You know we sent Apechi with them."

"Your soldiers don't know what they're doing in those ships." Speaker said, not unkindly. "Plus, don't Apechi have a tendency to . . . temporal and spatial confusion?"

"Caused by our god. Which has no reason to disrupt our pursuit of Daksha." Ming.

"It has no reason at all." Kis.

Ming glared.

"That we know of," Kis added. "Maybe it doesn't want us to find her. Speaker has a point. Although . . . I don't think it could hide Daksha from us if it wanted to. The confusions tend to be either temporary or . . . broadly conceptual. It doesn't do that kind of thing."

They contemplated their teas.

"Perhaps you should take some time off, Xar," Speaker suggested. "You look exhausted. And the Zetland is all but cleared."

"And Daksha isn't your problem, anyway. She's mine. I will deal with it, I will decide our next move." Ming attempted a look of concern. "Just relax for a while."

"It would be nice to have only one thing to worry about. Fucking stupid Ella. I wish I could kill him."

Speaker almost laughed. It was a remarkable thing, to be invaded and also privy to the complaints of the invader. After a long silence Speaker said, "If Daksha really is gone from Samfé, she'll be back. I'd wager she's already looking for us."

"Hm?" Both.

"The Zetland is no longer safe, and it has Vard in it."

"Surely not?" Ming smiled. "She cares that much?"

"You've lost me." Xar.

"Of course she does. I've just been telling you, she practically held the necromancer hostage after Vard died. If she's out there and not hiding in Samfé, she's out there looking for a way to bring him back."

"She can't do that, can she? Ming?"

"Surely not." Ming grinned. "I hope so though. I hope she's trying. Wouldn't that be fun. And"—she thumped the grass with excitement—"that means even less reason to worry about getting Vard out of the library. We can think of him as bait. Big juicy Daksha bait."

"Oh I don't like that at all." Xar's face showed this for a lie. "Good thinking, Speaker."

16

Firstly, we were on a lot of speed.

Medicinally of course—even Rhododendron had to be dosed. Our last emperor, walking into another empire's capital for help. Aren't you just captured by the poetry of it? No of course you're not. A normal audience would find it very moving. Will find it very moving, when I finally get around to reorganizing all this for publication. Perhaps even a screenplay. That's if your horrible god doesn't suddenly get bored of me and decide to turn me into one of these *tama*. You'll send my writing to an editor if it does, won't you? Ming please. Just say you will. Fine, fine.

We kept to our usual protocol. It was Rhododendron who insisted. He said that we're either Reds or we aren't, by which he meant that if we stopped following the rules of the empire we were trying to save then we would undermine the point of doing so. Which is fair enough but fuck. I mean, you've seen it out there. I'd rather leave the windows open for space-freaks than visit those people again.

The fucking architecture as well. I know it's very efficient and productive etcetera but it's like they're actively *trying* to look evil. As if they were at the design meeting or whatever saying, "You've heard of knives? Yes, give us those but gigantic and black with rivers of glowing slime." Slime aglow! And this is the people you've decided to be "allies" with.

Anyway, we'd had to dose ourselves with an amphetamine cocktail because the entire infernal planet hums. It's their god—which is also called fucking Ma can you believe it—it buzzes and vibrates. Absolutely perverse to be able to feel an actual living breathing deity the moment you set foot on the planet. It soothes the populace into this moron complacency which prevents any of them from caring that they live in a cult. But the drugs stopped it from getting to us, made its sensation annoying rather than relaxing. We learned that trick way back when Ma still came to the Olympic games, then it became our excuse for not letting the weird fuckers play.

We were escorted around by a group of priests. You can spot them a mile off because they wear ridiculous, glittery outfits with trinkets and bells dangling all over the place. They're trained to resist the god's attention, which means they remain clear-headed but have to distract it from everyone else in return. So really, if you think about it, they're all hostages.

Speaking of hostages, they did take us to see the real prisoners. You know, before the prophet turned them loose on the Zetland. It was abhorrent. Huge cages in the middle of their public spaces containing pitiful, sad shades of former glory. Deities hunted and captured from other worlds for their god's amusement. Miserable. And this from someone who thinks deities should all be destroyed. I still don't know why you believe that your god won't end up in one of those cages once the prophet manages to . . . manifest it or whatever she's told you she'll do. The locals see the trapped deities as trophies. They're proud. Avon seemed impressed. Kept asking how certain of them were captured. Ella may have behaved similarly if he wasn't already under house arrest at that point, but I hope not.

Some were beautiful though. There was one which looked like a cross between a snake and a fish, but with feathers. A snake fish bird. Such a beautiful animal. Every shade of red and silver, shimmering and floating on air. They had it in a long glass-looking dome, like a test tube upside down. An animal at the zoo. It had clever eyes. A mystery from another universe, an aberration, a virus. You're right that it doesn't matter what they really are. Whatever you think, there is something horrific about their presence. You just know that you're looking at something *else*.

The worst was one was a person. A human being, possessed and caged. You looked into his eyes and you saw the beginning of the world. Or the end. Or both. Rhododendron tried to speak to it, and it started following him around for some reason, fascinated by the shape of the necklace through Rhododendron's shirt. I wonder what it saw.

We assumed that we were making our way toward a formal meeting with the prophet, which we were, but it was at a stupid massive stadium. Absolute sadist of a woman decided we ought to go through another ordeal before begging her help. No wonder Xar likes her, she's like an old version of you. You are not welcome, that is not a compliment. No it isn't. Alright then. Denial is what you're in.

People were pouring into the stadium with us from all over the city. The hum was hauntingly audible, made it impossible to forget that the god was watching. I kept glancing up as if it lived in the sky.

Lucille was there, the fucking traitor. You'd think he'd have the decency to call in sick to whatever his job is on the one day that we're going to see him at it. Although I suppose someone like that would want to gloat. The prophet herself was really weird, obviously. We had the strangest conversation. There were these two people in protective suits not like the ones—

*

The invaders interrupted, laughing, and the life drained from Speaker's face. Downturned eyes cast wretched over their captors' smiles.

"Please don't. Please don't tell me that was you."

They laughed harder.

"You were already there? Oh fuck. Oh gods. I can't. I can't take it. We came straight to you."

"I'm afraid so," Xar said, frowning in a semblance of concern. "Have you only just realized? I assumed you knew. Where did you think we came from? You can't imagine how thrilled we were when you landed."

"It was already over before we arrived. This whole time I thought . . . I don't know. I don't know."

"Don't beat yourself up about it," Ming said.

"What the fuck. Were you waiting for us?"

"No. Weren't expecting you at all. In fact, we went for almost the same reason you did," Xar offered. "We needed help with our god. So did you. It's not that surprising we all had the same idea."

"I just can't . . . cope with this information. I don't think I can cope with this information." Speaker's face fell into their hands. "Fucking Avon fucking Stal. Fucking cunt. Stupid fucking cunt."

Ever seeing of the opportunities dangling ripe from despair Ming said, "She will get what's coming to her."

"You're going to find her?"

"Of course." Ming.

"How?" Speaker stood. "She's off the grid. She has more weapons than we do. Have you prepared the techs? Do we have Ma's crusaders on our side? You're wasting all those resources on Daksha, you need to concentrate on Avon."

"Avon cut her losses and fled. She made so many enemies over the century that we had plenty of planets willing to report sightings," Xar said, uninterested. "She's worlds away."

"She is far more dangerous to us than Daksha. Let's get her."

Us, thought Ming. She resisted the urge to glance smugly at Xar.

"Please not another thing. I only just had the chance to sit down." he said.

"It's fine, Xar. We can talk about this. I am open to the possibility that we focus more of our efforts on locating Avon and her ship."

"Yes!" Speaker.

"Ugh. I thought we were going to try to be friends with—"

Ming nudged Xar into silence. "Everybody knows you can't trust a traitor."

"Exactly." Speaker, suspiciously.

"It's too late to talk about this now. Let's have a break."

"Can't we have a permanent break?" Xar complained. "We can't get any more out of this biography thing. I'm sure of it. We've learned basically nothing. And I'm so very nearly through to Ella, we can just go back to the prophet for answers when we have him."

"What does she want him for?" Speaker.

"Cult reasons." Ming, quickly. "But look, forget all this for now, you reminded me of something, Speaker. Was Rhododendron wearing the necklace when he died?"

Speaker seemed winded by the question, steadied themself against their chair before they replied, "No. No I don't believe he would have been."

Ming smiled. "Then I think it's time we found it."

17

"You first, Speaker," she said, standing in the hallway outside Rhododendron's empty suite.

"It just feels wrong."

"Come on, you can do it." She considered placing a reassuring hand on their shoulder but decided that was a bridge too far.

"Please, Ming. This is hard enough without you suddenly acting like a human being."

Xar laughed. "Go on. I want in."

"Could you at least give me a moment in there alone?"

"What, so you can loot the good stuff? Not a chance." Xar.

"What good stuff? What are you expecting in there?"

"Go on." Ming's breath rattled through her mask.

Speaker accepted that it was time to obey. Their right shoe crossed the sliding door's track, settled in the forbidden space beyond. The emperor's twin stood in his suite for the first time since their mother's death. The air smelled like him. Incense, cedar, a hint of metal. It put Speaker on edge.

Using Speaker's second step as their cue, Ming and Xar took the room. Xar watched his hands touch things. The emperor's pen was fondled and rolled before it became an inmate of his pocket. Rhododendron's sofa was sat in. His desk ogled.

"It's not nearly as nice as your suite," commented Xar. "The furniture is more comfortable though."

"He was always in pain," said Ming, to Speaker's surprise. "He was too big, too modified. He must have wanted to collapse under the weight of himself. Am I right?"

Speaker nodded, unaffected by the thought of their brother's suffering. "Our mother said that it was to change the way people saw him, but I think it was to change him. He was not a calm child."

"What kind of person is soothed by discomfort?" asked Xar.

"One trained to believe that denial is improvement," Ming answered. "That sacrifice is always good."

Speaker watched her. They weren't sure if they were hearing a misguided criticism of the Red faction, a personal manifesto, or nonsense designed to interest Xar. It did not occur to Speaker that part of Ming's obsession models her after Rhododendron. "His bedroom is the second door over there," they said, "which is where the necklace will be, if it's here."

Ming was the first to enter. The room was very different from the one they had left behind, which seemed like a staff room. The emperor's bedroom was soft, dark, heavy with rugs and huge pieces of drooping furniture. There was a disco ball. They all stared at the disco ball.

"What is that?" asked Xar.

"Disco ball," Ming said, curiously.

"What the hell is a disco ball? And don't say 'that.' I know it's that."

"It scatters light around the room. It's decorative." Speaker was still watching it, as if it too were an intruder in the space.

"I assume you agree that the disco ball is an unexpected feature, Speaker?" Ming stalked over to Rhododendron's gigantic bed and opened the cabinet to its side.

"Um. Yes."

"I want to see this disk ball," Xar said. "Control panel? The one by the door?"

"Probably." Speaker.

"Here." Ming turned, her hand raised. A small, thin chain dangled between her fingers. At its end swung a pendulum of scrap metal, a shittily wrought relic handed down from revolutionaries long dead. It slowed and span, showing off rough edges as they swayed back and forth. Speaker walked toward her, watching it sadly all the while.

"What would they say, if they could see all this? The first Reds I mean. If they could see the last hundred years, even. Everything they went through." Speaker sighed. "We let them down. We've been letting them down for a long time."

Ming raised her palm, letting the symbol hang at the end of its chain. "Take it."

"What?"

"It's yours," she said. "It was your mother's and then it was his. It's yours."

"I don't . . . I can't. I don't deserve it."

"Perhaps it will remind you to try." She lowered her hand so that the loop of chain would slip over her fingertips. Speaker caught it. "Good. Put it on."

Speckles of light flooded the room, multicolored stars rotating into the corners. There was music, a thudding techno beat with a woman's voice an ethereal lullaby over the top. They all looked up at the disco ball, but it wasn't spinning.

"Wrong switch!" shouted Speaker over the sound, "You've turned on a holo!"

But Xar's attention was focused on the other side of the room. He grinned, jabbed at the control panel again to pause. "Look!"

Rhododendron's holo sat naked on the sofa, surrounded by beautiful, similarly attired people.

"No way." Ming was among the ghosts immediately, removing her mask, eyes wild with delight. "Is this expiate? No, cocaine." A tube of liquid ran through a young woman's hands into Rhododendron's neck. "Shit, they've got so much going on over here—where is it all? It must still be in here."

"No, no." Speaker stood on Rhododendron's other side, eyes fixed on their brother. "This can't be real. It can't be. Is he drinking? Is that rum? I don't believe it."

"He never invited you to his parties?" Xar asked.

"He didn't have parties!"

"Clearly did." Ming laughed. "Fuck, look, there's still a pipe over here. Xar, press play, come on! Let's see what he recorded."

"No, no." Speaker, again.

The music played, the lights span around an immobile disco ball. The young woman to Rhododendron's left unscrewed the pipe from his neck, tapped it off, licked the hole it left on him before sliding the steel around to seal it again. The emperor rolled his eyes with excitement as the drug hit and kissed the woman to his right. She grabbed his dick. Speaker screamed.

"Look at the size of it!" Xar, in awe. "Who is this one? He's beautiful."

The man in question clambered over the coffee table, knocked bottles out of his way with hammered dexterity in eagerness to join. Rhododendron seized his throat, poured rum into his gaping mouth before standing to follow it with his cock.

Speaker tried to turn around, leave the room. Xar blocked. "No."

They watched Rhododendron pound the kneeling man's face, push him away, pick up one of the two women. He carried her through Speaker and Xar, tossed her onto the bed where she laughed, turned onto her back, spread her legs. He grabbed her ankles and pulled her to the edge of the mattress.

Xar pushed Speaker over to them, gently, then with more force as the steward tried to resist. "Take off that suit," he said.

"What? No."

Xar broke the clasp at Speaker's waist, pushed them down onto the bed with both hands until they were laying over the woman's holo. Rhododendron knelt to lick her cunt.

"Stop it."

Xar split Speaker's thighs and grinned at Ming, who climbed onto the bed to say, "Don't struggle, unless you want me to hold you down."

"No!"

"Let it happen," she whispered, lying prone so her lips could touch Speaker's ear. "It's okay."

Xar spat into the palm of his hand. Rhododendron's ghost stood, leaning over the young woman, turning he and Xar into one—a chimera of the emperor and the man who killed him, their faces melting in and out of each other with identical expressions of pleasure.

"Yes," Xar hissed, while Rhododendron's lips moaned beneath his. "Look at me."

"How does it feel?" Ming, taking Speaker's hand and coaxing it into her skirt.

Speaker gasped as Xar plunged into them, raised their hips, sunk the tip of their finger into the wet slit of Ming's cunt.

18

Ella was happy to see me. We really had become a lot closer since the whole Samfé affair. He didn't deserve to be locked up like that, even if it was only in his own apartment. Fucking Avon Stal.

I don't know what he was thinking, he didn't have nearly enough support to overwhelm her. I took him one of my favorite vodkas and some vermouth. Had to drink it out of little flute glasses because that's all he had.

"Women love it, darling," is how he justified this. "They think I'm a sweet little baby with strange affectations. Silly man who drinks only sparkling wine."

We were sitting on his bedroom floor and watching space rotate beyond his window. Huge semicircular pane of glass, gorgeous thing. Not sure how they keep the freaks away from it.

"You seem to devote a lot of your energies to making women like you." I shouldn't have said that really, he was arrested for goodness' sake. You don't need criticism when you've already done a failed coup. Was it a coup? Oh I don't know. We were acting like it wasn't in order to keep everybody calm, but it would have been a coup in normal times. He took it well anyway.

"I find that making a game of life serves as an excellent distraction from that fact of it."

He was right about that. I asked, "How are you going to distract yourself now?"

"Well darling, I expect I can enjoy these nice visits with those of you who haven't shunned me for my regrettable episode. Other than that I'll dwell on my mistakes and learn either to hate myself or not to make them again when this plan of hers inevitably dooms us all."

I laughed. "What do you think you did wrong, then?"

"I should've killed her, Speaker. Don't worry, I won't try to convince you to do the same. But I am being quite serious. I should have killed her. She should be dead."

That was technically treason, of course. She was the acting Military emperor now he was locked up. But it didn't feel dangerous to talk to him about it so I said, "Why didn't you?"

"You know, darling, it's the strangest thing. I meant to. I was going to. I just . . . at the final moment I was overcome with this feeling. And I know this sounds insane but I also know that our little chats stay between us so I shall tell you anyway. I was overcome with this feeling that it would be a bad idea. Not even a feeling, I was certain. I just knew. It was like a sort of . . . opposite déjà vu. Not seeing something which has already happened, but something that is absolutely, conclusively going to happen."

"Like a vision?"

"No, nothing like that. I just suddenly knew how I was going to feel once she was dead, that something worse was going to happen if I succeeded." He shrugged. "I bet she has some sort of pheromone in her bioware which releases if you get too close, stops you from wanting to hurt her."

*

"Why are you showing me this?" asked Xar, putting down the pad which Ming had handed to him.

Speaker looked over from their canvas. "What is it?"

"The section of your memoir—"

"Debut auto-fictional endeavor."

"The section of your debut auto-fictional endeavor," Ming corrected herself, "where you went to visit Ella."

"Oh? Do you like it? I think it's becoming a fine psychological portrait. Needs tuning of course. I'm hoping an editor has some good notes in that regard when I finally settle on one. Ella deserves my best writing."

"Is it true, though?" she asked.

"Of course."

"This stuff about déjà vu, he definitely said that?"

"Yes."

"Ah . . ." Kis breathed, "I see what you're thinking."

"Fill me in."

"Ella's infected," she said. "It told him not to kill Avon in the same way it told you to kill Clara. I'm right. The prophet's right." There was no triumph in her tone, no excitement either. "It found you both and it's keeping you both alive. I'm right."

Speaker's eyebrows met in confusion. "No, can't be. He was . . . he had his shirt off that whole time, no spines nor scars from them."

"That's not impossible," said Xar. "Remember Keh Niko? She only ever grew them in her gums when we were kids. Not a mark on her." His mouth turned into a smug smile, "It got me everywhere though."

"It might even have . . . I mean why couldn't it be on his legs or in his hair? And, and, if I'm right—which I am—then it might have tried not to show itself in him at all."

"Why would it bother to conceal itself in him but not me?" Speaker.

"Because he would have turned himself in, Speaker. He would have confessed, put himself in the medical wing, and been killed for it. You're a coward so it didn't bother. The god is keeping you both alive. This is it. We've been right all along. It's all here. It wasn't a trick. It wants us to talk to it."

Xar nodded, uninterested. "Fine. Why not? It's what we're doing anyway."

"What are you both talking about? I'm sick of being in the dark here, tell me what's going on." Speaker.

"If you're so sure," began Xar, ignoring Speaker, "then I should be able to break into the Military wing and drag the fucker out. If it's keeping him alive then we have nothing to worry about. It won't let him poison himself or let me accidentally punch through his face."

Ming's expression hardened above her mask. "Mistakes happen. It's too risky."

"You're not sure," he goaded her. "You're just bored."

"What if it turns us both into *tama*?" Speaker whined, sounding like they had been trying not to ask this. "What if that's its plan, just weaken the government from the top down."

"Can't believe you're still worried about that. Never should've told you." Kis.

"Of course I'm still worried about that. You said it turned people into a 'walking coma.' Mindless."

"Yes but it only happens to . . ." Ming looked to Xar for help.

"Dregs," he supplied. "And while you are very annoying, you do have skills. You aren't an abject loser. Plus, Ella definitely isn't."

"How do you know it does that?" Speaker, pleading. "Do you actually *know* that it chooses which people to destroy based on skill or do you just assume that because it didn't choose you?"

"Commander!" someone yelled, bursting through the trees in a Military uniform.

"Noo," Xar groaned, turning in the soldier's direction. "What?"

Panting, the Military-uniformed man said, "'nother godthing, in vents by library. Need help."

"Fuck's sake." Ming.

"I thought you killed them all?" Speaker.

"So did I. Fine, fine. Coming." Xar pointed at a few of his guards to follow as he jogged after the young man.

"See what listening to that prophet gets you?"

"Speaker, imagine for me a moment how much bloodshed there would have been without her. The godthings are a pain to get back out of here obviously but the psychological effect of their invasion certainly saved thousands of lives. The Zetland surrendered so quickly."

"You don't care." Speaker.

"Yes, I do. You think I want power over ruins?"

Speaker nodded to indicate a decorative column poking out of the dirt in their clearing. "You have it."

"I told you we will replace those as soon as you tell me what with. Do I look like a landscape architect?"

"I said more trees!"

"Well you should've said it when I was listening." Ming.

"Listen." Speaker.

"I am."

"No. Shh. Listen."

Ming realized from Speaker's distant expression that they were not focusing on her. She listened.

The guards reacted a moment faster. Gunshots, screams. Somewhere in the garden itself.

"Stay," yelled a guard, in Crysthian, turning back to Speaker and Ming, "hide."

Ming obeyed, holding an arm out to grab Speaker—who was still trying to run to Xar in panic.

The two of them backed away to the far side of the trees. Behind the trunks, in the undergrowth. More gunshots.

"Fuck," Ming hissed, "your fucking easel. They'll know we're here."

"Is it Ella?"

"Of course it's fucking Ella."

Speaker found this less comforting than they might have a few months prior. Ming unclasped her shirt and pulled out a seeking knife.

"Do you have a spare?" they asked.

"No," she answered.

"Shit."

"It's fine. We'll be fine."

"They lured Xar away on purpose, didn't they?" Speaker.

"Yes."

"Shit."

They were in a far corner of the gardens. Densely forested enough to provide the illusion of real solitude. Hidden but also trapped. The attack could not have come at a better time. She began to use fantasies of future revenge to distract herself from present fear.

"Mina?" A woman's voice, from the clearing. "Mina, we know you're here. Just come out."

It took Speaker a moment to remember that this was Ming's name. They looked over at her, mouthed, "Adora?"

Ming nodded, face unreadable. Mostly because of the mask. She held a finger to her metal lips.

"Mina, please." The voice cracked. "Let us take you alive."

Speaker nodded vigorously. Ming shook her head.

"Let's just give ourselves up, see what happens."

"No," Ming hissed back, "you will help me fight, you little fucker."

"How?"

She lowered herself as close to the ground as possible and peered around the trunk of her tree. She said, "It's only Adora and Haja. Haja's wounded. If they'd won there'd be more of them. I can still hear gunshots. They've run ahead alone."

"So what do we do?"

"Mina! Please! You don't have to do this anymore."

"You run. That way. Distract Haja." Ming.

"What? No!"

"Now! Now! Go—I will fucking stab you myself—go!"

Speaker ran. Neither of the two women shot as neither were trained with the aim-assisted pistols they were using. Adora was desperate to defend her daughter, defend herself, still holding out hope that she might discover this all a mistake.

Ming flicked her thumb up the seeking blade to activate it, her eyes fixed on Adora's throat. She felt a subdermal implant tremble in her arm to show her it was ready, target locked. She ran into the clearing, released the blade.

Haja screamed and shot, missed, hadn't even tried to engage the pistol's assist. Adora bled on steel. Speaker did nothing.

Slick with blood the seeking knife sought to return to its master's fingers but the signal was weakened by something in Adora's bioware. Nothing in her had been designed for war and the healing web of her skin which usually resolved scratches and bruises was latching to the knife. The weapon freed itself anyway but collapsed to the ground, out of power. Ming threw herself at Haja, grabbing her wrist. Haja was old, Ming debilitated by compulsive self-mutilation.

"Speaker!" Ming yelled, trying to remain standing, to not let the older woman push her to the ground. "Speaker! Help me!"

Speaker emerged from the trees, ran over to Adora, held their hands to her throat. Nothing would help. Hemorrhaging beneath the superficial repair to her skin. Adora's prosthetic fingers closed around Speaker's wrists. She could not talk, she could not breathe.

A thud to the right and Haja was on top of Ming, trying to bend the pistol to her face. She had discovered that Ming had something wrong with her ribs. She pressed her knee to the younger's woman's side. Ming screaming, trying to push the weapon away, failing.

Speaker freed their arms from Adora's dying grip, scrambled over to the knife.

"Speaker! Yes!" Haja cried, triumphant.

Ming's eyes widened.

Speaker slit her throat, horrified, shrieking, not daring to break eye contact as they stared at each other in mutual shock.

Gunshots in the distance, the fight raged on.

Ming's arms fell to her sides. Gasping through the mask. Rattling in hideous desperation for air. She closed her eyes. Speaker pushed Haja away, freeing Ming's wounded torso from the weight of her.

"I'm so sorry. I'm so sorry," Speaker kept repeating, looking into Haja's eyes. "I'm so sorry."

Ming's ragged lips touched the cold metal as she smiled, still in agony, still breathless.

She had won. Again.

Speaker crawled over to her, "Are you hurt?"

Ming's body tried to laugh, but her ribs rebelled.

Haja bled her life into the grass.

Xar barrelled back through the trees, Crysthian gun in one hand, head bleeding. "Ming!" he wailed, seeing her on the ground, dress shining with wet blood.

Speaker had never seen his face like that before. The god was pouring into him, doing what it does. He was a blur of texture, shadows of him lurching around his body, becoming animal, becoming human. He lifted the gun to Speaker's face.

"She's alive! She's fine!" they yelled, holding up their red hands.

Kaleidoscopic with sacred hallucination Xar fell to his knees, touched Ming's face, saw the smile in her eyes.

"Ella," she whispered. "Go for him, go now."

PART II

The Prophet

19

Flowers bloom on the prophet's skin where her god adores her. The deity kneads in naïve curiosity; a baby's devotion, ever on the edge of violence because it does not know what violence is. Little flowers, almost like stars. Her suit keeps the worst of it away.

Members of Ma's ecclesiastical class are covered in trinkets. Silver dangling ornaments which reflect the light, distract the god's attention, give it things to play with. These people are born with a natural resistance to the Ma hum, but there's nothing magical about their peculiarity. They are just impatient, stubborn, quick to anger—possessed of a personality that doesn't easily fall into contentment. Their nature gives them the ability to make out the god Ma's edges, prevent it from naturalizing and disappearing into their lives, never to be seen again. A constant, physical reification as the god's soothing hum ricochets from the veil of their annoyance. Ma swipes at the theocrats as they go about their governance, excited by their shimmering armor.

The prophet is not like her priests. She can see into the god, feel its drives, its moods. Not that it has any of these things. It does not talk through her because it cannot speak and wouldn't if it could but she knows how to shepherd it, keep it satisfied. It loves chasing other deities but it knows that human bodies are full of stringy, squishy toys. It knows how they scream and run. She makes sure it gets its special treats.

Ma the deity gives U6-93 no extraordinary powers in herself. Only the right to rule, which naturally accompanies her ability to control the empire's one perfect weapon. She does care for her people. She is aging, and she fears that she will die before she finds a replacement, someone else who can keep Ma's innocent violence facing outward. That is what the stadium is for.

"Arrived, have they, these seekers of my skill?" she asked in the lingering, bony words of Ma's language.

"Yes. The Red emperor, his steward, and Avon Stal," answered Lucille. He spoke Ma with a heavy Crysthian accent, even after all these years. "There are a few bishops with them in the box."

The prophet picked up her crown, a silver chandelier. "They have created a world in which three can be so brittle." she said.

"I'll be translating for you, I assume?"

"Of course."

"They won't like that."

"Of course."

Lucille smirked, lifted his thin robotic forearms to help her with the crown. This is a man who has undergone amputation twice—once to gain the black hands of the Crysthian ambassadorial class, once again to lose them when his allegiance shifted to the Ma empire.

The stadium roared when the prophet arrived. Her people could not see her but they could feel the attention of Ma itself as it followed her, its hum concentrating wherever she walked and flowing around the crowd with a kneading, molten euphoria.

Crysth waited. Rhododendron standing like an embarrassed teenager with his arms folded around him. His bioware gleamed through a high-necked shirt which had been tailored in Crysth's formal style, its fabric left translucent that his modifications might be better seen beneath it. He raised his arm as he turned them off, one at a time, the landscape of his body cooling like an urban sunrise. Speaker lurked slender behind him, painted face raised slightly to the ceiling, eyebrow cocked.

"Her Holiness U6-93, ambassador Lucille," announced a glimmering bishop as she opened the door.

Avon Stal jumped up from the couch to greet them. Transferring a glass of bubbling spirit to her left hand and grasping the prophet's palm with her right she said, "U6-93."

"Please, you are a general who has harried my forces, tormented my borders, and been known to me as greater than friend. Placing such formality between us with all these things true does nothing but appear as a slight to the respect of our mutual animosity. Worse it appears as a form of manifest self-disregard, a denial, a childish avoidance of the fact of our relationship." The prophet's silver teeth showed beneath her crown. "Call me Dash."

Avon understood only the final sentence. She said, "Hello again, Dash. It has been too long. And Lucille, I see you've kept the epithet. What exactly are you the ambassador of?"

"Hope," he replied in a tone of disconcerting sincerity, "the notion that we can overcome decades of propaganda and create ourselves anew."

"Perverse," said Speaker.

"You are a treacherous clown and your presence here is offensive." Rhododendron.

"Guests," began the prophet, "my knowledge of your tongue limited though it is I can reckon but from your expressions and your tone that the attendance of my highly regarded advisor is here interpreted as maliciousness on our part. This is not so. I require—as I tell you now about me that I find automatic translation invasive, untrustworthy, most rotten of all distracting—a human being to put into your words the meaning of mine. We are in possession of others with the skill but not so with the talent as Lucille, whose remarkability lies not in linguistics but his proximity to and therefore intimacy with me. I trust that he knows greatest among my court what I mean when I speak."

"She says I'm her translator and I'm best at it," provided Lucille.

"Wh . . . what else did she say?" Speaker.

"Please," Avon interjected, "we'll be here all day long."

The prophet extended an upturned palm at shoulder height in the direction of the assembled black hands and Military captains, the Ma equivalent of a wave. "I beg of you to make yourselves comfortable among my clergy. There is food and drink here served to you but I notice the general is alone in your cohort in trusting that I have not taken upon myself to poison it."

"Enjoy the buffet," said Lucille. To Avon alone he said, "She notices that you trusted she wouldn't poison you."

The general smiled. "And I notice that she remembered my favorite cocktail. But no, I don't trust shit. The implants in my fingers alert me to toxicity in anything I am holding." The two women laughed as they went together to a long black sofa. There was a cushion to its left which was obviously intended for Rhododendron. He took it with bad grace.

"Your Holiness," a bishop, hand up to inspect a screen which only she could see, "I'm messaging the candidates, shall we delay the start?"

"A delay is to be expected at an event such as this and therefore is no delay at all. They will have a short while longer, tell them so," she replied.

Lucille told the Crysthians what had been said and then added, "See how much easier things are when you allow people to have personal communication devices?"

"You know what happened, Lucille." Rhododendron, sternly.

"The disaster on Earth was not the fault of the devices, rather the environment of the people using them."

"Can we debate Crysthian history another time?" Avon suggested.

"This is not Crysthian history. Crysth did not exist. Herein lies your problem. You people even colonize time."

"What is the use of dividing history into pieces? Everything that has ever happened has brought us here." Rhododendron.

"That doesn't make it yours." Lucille, no longer translating but just arguing with his former masters.

"It exactly does." Rhododendron.

"Oh shut up," said Avon. "Stop bickering before someone says something irretractable like 'autopoiesis' or 'Deleuze.'"

In the distance afforded by her incomprehension, U6-93 had turned her attention to Speaker. Looking them up and down, eyes fixing on their chest. A smile crossing her lips. Speaker had noticed this but was trying to pretend they hadn't.

"You are Speaker," observed U6-93, curiously. Lucille cut himself off mid-sentence to translate for her. "How are you feeling?"

They all turned to Speaker, who, horrified, responded with: "How are *you* feeling?"

"Dammit, Speaker," whispered the emperor.

"Can you sense Ma's mighty hum?" she asked. "Can you feel her?"

"Of course. We all can."

She tilted her head to the side, draping her ornaments entirely out of the way of her silver-tattooed eyes to scrutinise the steward. "Is it so? Another time perhaps I will press upon you for more of the feeling for I sense even that you yourself have another experience altogether of this place. Although I could, a lifelong devotee of my one dear Ma, be quite wrong.

"But, to center myself in the present moment and if you'll permit me to be rudely direct, I tell you that I know exactly why you all have come. Ill news travels fast even over the stars and even among peoples who hold each other at a careful distance such as we. And I want to be clear that I mean no sarcasm no mockery by the term 'ill news' for it is indeed ill to me to hear of your present misfortune—predictable though it may be. Any instability among the planets and the peoples who infest upon them is of no benefit to Ma, but you must mistake not pity regarding the fact of your demise for pity in its method. This creature of Apech's seems designed perfect for your destruction, and I hope you take it upon yourselves with what time you have left to ponder this. It is perhaps not too late to repent. You cannot, I tell you now as I have told you always, resist that which you refuse to acknowledge."

Smirking, Lucille translated: "The prophet regrets how screwed you all are but suggests there may be hope."

Avon raised a hand to silence the short-tempered emperor before she said, "We have come here to seek your counsel, Dash, as I'm sure you well know."

"Avon says," began Lucille in Ma, "that they want your advice."

"And I shall give it. But you find me here on a festival day, and so you must first do me the courtesy of enjoying it. Please, be at home."

"Thank you, Dash. I'm sure the festivities will be a welcome break from this being invaded we're having." Avon lifted her glass to the prophet, who took it. She spun its delicate stem in her fingers until the stain of Avon's lipstick faced her mouth and there drank from it.

"Does it taste as you remembered?" Avon asked.

Without waiting for a translation, U6-93 said, "No."

20

Beneath the crowd's feet, a dramaturgical hiss as the pipes shuddered into life.

Ma's residents howled with anticipation. Between the stands, valves began to whisper mist into the air over their heads. Holy water. Pure standard H_2O—but they don't need to know that.

They roared, lifting their faces their tongues to taste the sacred air. Clapping and screaming as their prophet stepped onto her balcony, raised her hands to greet them.

Her crown towered above her in asymmetrical branches of silver, tchotchkes dangled from every inch. Beneath her chin her armor shimmered, a catastrophe of bulging metal, a suit made of gifts given by those lucky enough to have met her. A key from a child with outstanding musical ability, a thimble from a woman who had lived to one hundred. These lucky souls scrolled through videos of U6-93's public appearances thereafter, trying to spot their fetish among all those that adorned her. Screenshot, zoom in, draw an arrow before posting online. Praise Ma.

Her face was enlarged over the screen at the stadium's center. The Crysthians stared at it, then tried not to see it at all—offended by its ostentatious, invasive vulgarity. How dare it take their image somewhere they hadn't been themselves? They all realized with discomfort that they were being photographed and recorded by thousands in the stands.

Rhododendron activated his facial bioware, hiding himself behind the lights.

The show began. Music, dancing, miscellaneous hyping of the crowd. Overhead the cool mist kept the god rapt with something like fascinated terror—preventing Ma from attacking the performers as they vaulted and waved.

Tension rose. Around the perimeter of the arena thirty-two circles of light became brighter as the main event neared. The people watched them, cheering as their edges solidified into cracks in the floor.

Above, the valves' susurration quietened as the mist withdrew, covering only the spectators so that Ma's interest could be allowed to roam into the arena.

Darkness but for the circles of light. Drums.

The lights strobed with the beat. Standing on rising columns which brought them almost to the height of the crowd, the contenders ignored the stadium, concentrated. The floor fell away and from it emerged an obstacle course. Sharp things, deep things, a network of entertaining ruin and the targets at its center. A race: five targets, five winners.

Despite the horrors of the arena already in evidence, the greatest obstacle to victory was Ma itself. Delighted by the blood and the running and the anxiety, the god will join in.

Over the loudspeaker, a cardinal introduced the competitors to the audience. The crowd knew them already. Celebrities, bishops who were brave bold ferocious enough to fight for advancement to the higher court. The cardinals have stood before Ma alone and lived.

On U6-93's balcony, the Crysthians could not understand the introductions but they could tell which of the bishops were crowd favorites by the ebb and flow of noise. A very muscular, scantily clad woman with a mace and red tattoos earned a particular roar. Another for a barrel-armored man whose only weapon appeared to be a glowing cylinder the size of a tennis ball. A strangely haunted cry for a young bishop with one arm. The injury seemed recent, still heavily bandaged.

Silence. The bishops knelt, the crowd stood. Six final platforms rose. Six waiting bodies for Ma to control. Heaps of fur. Beasts bred to be deified, drugged into dreamless sleep. Ma can wield air and so it did not need these, but manifestation makes for a better spectacle.

The lights returned, the stadium erupted, attention focused back on the bishops. U6-93 leaned into her microphone and there said: you may begin.

Many of the contestants started to communicate with each other. Years of training led to this. They had formed allegiances and plans. Their placement on the circuit was random and so those who had chosen to navigate the course together must first reach one another. There could only be five winners but teams were infrequently less than seven; they knew they would lose some on the way.

Navigating both the physical challenges of the arena and one another, the contestants danced through the pitch. Some, especially those making solo bids, began to fight one another. The tattooed woman swung her mace into a man's chest and sent him and his crossbow careening into the waiting spikes below. The crowd screamed in disappointment or glory as a camera drone zoomed in on the carnage. Action replay, live stream of the fluctuating odds.

The beasts began to stir. The contestants were not looking but they could tell from the noise of the crowd that yellow eyes were opening, claws stretching, tails twitching into sacred locomotion.

A drone flew down to focus on the man with the cylinder of light. His progress had been odd, the only contestant to move toward the animals rather than the maze's center. The crowd screamed as he leapt onto a platform beside one of the spotted cats, lowering himself to the ground and moving crabwise with the device hidden behind his back. Ma's creature woke, he grabbed its attention before showing it the light, rolling it, making it disappear again. A yo-yo. The yellows of the creature's eyes narrowed as the black pupils swallowed them, focused. The man kept playing, teasing, distracting, glancing over to the other cats as he did. He could only handle one at a time. His plan will fail immediately and spectacularly unless he can enact it quickly, and unless the other godthings are distracted when he does.

Elsewhere the one-armed man died beneath Ma's corporeal paws. The crowd's applause was his benediction. He had not tried to fight. He died redeemed.

The tattooed woman was losing the crowd's favor. Too bloodthirsty perhaps—her strategy didn't seem to extend beyond murdering the competition.

Ma sent a tigerbody prancing into the fray between two teams. Those with larger weapons attempted to dismember it. Ma within could not feel pain, but the body could be torn apart. Interhuman dispute forgotten as both teams cooperated to destroy the pony-sized cat.

Back on a creature plinth the yo-yoer was running out of time to perform his trick. Exhausted, blinking sweat from his eyes.

He did it, released the yo-yo in front of the creature's face and in a movement practiced countless times on running horses he mounted the sacred flesh. Rubber pads on the inside of his armored legs, left hand bunched around fur.

He had endured months of insomnia as he convinced himself that this plan might work—yet he still could not believe that it actually had. Nor could the crowd. They had never been louder.

As he had predicted, Ma's animal lost all interest in the yo-yo once he was on its back. It rolled to dislodge or crush him, but it wasn't heavy enough to crack the barrel of his armor. When it tires of resistance he will let the yo-yo loose, lure the creature ridiculous to victory. An unwilling anglerfish, following a lasso of light. He will be one of the five winners.

"Are you seeing this shit?" called Avon Stal. "I bet I could do that."

"No, you couldn't," smiled the prophet. "My lovely and brutal Ma would crush you with air if you were to step into that arena. The contestants can feel her, almost like I can. Hopefully one day exactly like I can. They know how not to die."

Lucille translated.

Speaker stepped back from the balcony's railing to ask, "You're sure it's safe here? There's a couple down there wearing black suits which look to me rather like protective gear. Should we be wearing protective gear?"

"I do believe you should, it is very interesting to me that you in particular are still alive. Ma is a solitary creature." Lucille did not translate because he did not understand what she meant. But she said it kindly so Speaker took it as a no.

The prophet stood to join Speaker, hulking over them in the melting monstrosity of her attire. With only her filed teeth visible she spoke nonsense sounds and Lucille translated, "Look at the man in the black suit. Do you recognise him as your kin?"

Obedient even in disgust Speaker glanced back at the man on the balcony beneath them before saying, "I have no kin but the Red emperor."

"I wonder if the costume prevents your identification, designed to contain as well as deflect. Look at him."

A surge of noise from the crowd, which Rhododendron used as an excuse to intervene in the conversation. "What happened in the arena?" he asked.

"My first winner," she sighed. "A . . . yo-yoer."

Speaker agreed with an empathetic frown. "I'm afraid it is a yo-yoer, yes."

"Seems clever to me," Rhododendron said. "A good way not to die."

"Wouldn't you be ashamed to live in such a way?" Lucille translated, after a medium-length monologue from the prophet's lips.

"Yes." Speaker.

"I would be more ashamed by the vanity implied in not doing so." Rhododendron.

Lucille narrowed his eyes then said to the prophet, "I think the emperor says that it would be more embarrassing to die because you were too embarrassed to use the yo-yo than to live because you used the yo-yo. Get it?"

"Ahh . . . he assumes we all feel deep down that life, not glory, is the ultimate prize but must pretend that we do not. In your philosophy the greatest aim is therefore not to be found in the pursuit of glory but in the act of dropping glory's pretense."

"She says that you think that air is better than honor." Lucille. This is not as poor a translation as it seems on a linguistic level, the Ma word for life is parallel to its word for breathing.

"I am a materialist." Rhododendron.

Lucille rolled his eyes as he translated and then asked Rhododendron, "How do you reconcile such a thing with a world of magic?"

"It wouldn't matter either way but it isn't magic," he answered. "You know it isn't magic."

Lucille said, "Are you sure you want me to say that to her?"

"Yes."

He did. She smiled her silver lips and said no more. Down in the arena, a second victor had achieved the central podium.

21

Jingle jangle said the prophet's suit as her cardinals followed her from the stadium.

"That went well," observed Lucille.

"By which you mean the meeting with our friends from Crysth or the festival itself I do not know, but I share your sentiment in neither case. My five new archbishops are skilled warriors, clever manipulators. But they are not cardinals. I allow myself to hope that the two greatest among them may learn, but I fear the ability must be innate."

"If I may," began a cardinal, "I would suggest that the festival forces such an impression upon its observer."

"Go on."

"It compels them to compete and in so doing acts as an incidental disservice to its victorious. By this I mean no criticism; I know that Ma enjoys the scene, and I know that our holy armies will not crusade behind a cardinal who cannot fight. I merely state that the necessity of survival obliges otherwise highly capable people to perform parlor tricks rather than to behave in a way more befitting of a higher holy order."

"You're referring to F42-SR," said another.

"I believe he is talented, despite the vulgar puppetry we saw today. He played Ma like an animal because an animal Ma was being. The daring of such a risk suggests higher sensitivity than the format of the game allows."

"You mean to say," the prophet said, "that just because his understanding of Ma as huntercat was all we saw, does not mean that is all he has to show?"

The cardinal did not answer; it is a linguistic idiosyncrasy of Ma to consent with silence. An unusually barren habit for a language prone to verbose postulation, Ma's wild vacillation between austerity and abundance makes Crysthian seem silly to them in comparison, a clucking language operating more like a game than actual communication.

"But why do you think the meeting went poorly?" Lucille, impatient.

"I am surprised that you do not. Perhaps you are showing me too much pleasure in their demise. It brings me no joy to look upon the doomed as they stand before me, to know I am lying by omission to their faces as they sit comfortably beside me. Part of me wants to capture them, keep them in cages like unhappy wild things, too tame to live in the jungle and too beautiful to be allowed to try. It will be a waste of them if they choose to perish. The general, I hope, will have the sense to flee. It seems the Ethicist already has, although we must check with Samfé."

"We are uncertain that the white wing of the Zetland is still in Samfé?" A cardinal. "I will text them and ask."

"It's called pearl, not white," corrected Lucille. Nobody cared. "I'm surprised you pity them."

"I am nearing retirement," she said. "It is preemptive nostalgia for the enemy of my youth."

They rounded a corner, descended.

A cardinal raised their hand in a motion indicating they had received a text message and then said, "The Apechi commanders are waiting for us at home already."

The vehicle which awaited them was, like much of Ma's design, triangular. The country's architecture was characterized by tall, irregular, slanted pyramids which jutted from the ground like gemstones. Falling over each other, overlapping in a natural, tectonic excitement. The ship looked like a chip of stone.

Behind closed doors in the rooms above their cathedral, each cardinal placed their armor onto a mannequin designed for them. All suits were silver but none alike beyond. Spikes, wings, horns. The sleekest seemed a costume of the ocean's surface. The most absurd had batwings made of umbrella-like arms which folded away when its wearer tired of the effect.

Undressed and slouching, the cardinals were still marked as agents of Ma. Sharpened silver teeth, silver eyes, shimmering runic tattoos.

Lucille shook the trinkets from the slender pipes of his forearms and said, "Apech is waiting for us in the astronomy lab."

"There is too much eagerness about them. An anxiety," commented a cardinal.

"I do not blame them for it. Their enemy is here. Their god is rogue. To not be anxious would suggest foolishness," another said.

"They know not the name of their own god. They are irreverent." This is a bad word, spoken from the cardinal with the bat suit. He is the greatest of them, the prophet calls him Fivepoint.

"No," U6-93 began. "They are ignorant. They have risked much in their coming, they are ready to make sacrifice. That is not irreverence. More importantly and whatever their own god does, Ma has taken a liking to it. You have seen this. Did you notice that it is inside the Red emperor's steward?"

"What?" Lucille, following her up the stairs.

"You heard. And whatever possesses the steward is on its best behavior. As if it knows where it is, as if it is aware of Ma and so keeps itself tame and secret and gentle in submission to her. This is very interesting to me. Ma is a solitary creature. But she has not made any motions like she wants to attack any of our Apechi visitors."

"She . . . likes the Apechi god?" Lucille.

"I truly believe she does."

A cardinal skipped forward to open the doors before them, letting U6-93 into the room. Glass ceiling, tiled floors for easy cleaning. Cult astronomy gets messy. At its center lay two unconscious Apechi soldiers, hands entwined. Xar Kis and Wilhelmina Ming waited at the room's farthest corner. They were out of their own protective suits, unnecessary within the cathedral's lopsided spike.

"Dash, Fivepoint," greeted Xar, who remained seated so as not to disturb the fluffy cat in his lap. It was the first house cat he had ever seen and he adored it.

Ming radiated apprehension.

Both the prophet and her cardinals stopped in their tracks, staring at the cat.

Eventually Lucille said, "Are you aware that you're stroking Ma's chin?"

"Hmm?" he asked, then looked down at the creature. It blinked slowly up at him before digging its tiny claws into his forearm with vibrating pleasure. "Aww. Are you god? Ming. Look. It's god."

Ming let out an exhalation of breath that was almost a laugh. "Are we to understand that this is the source of Ma?"

After Lucille translated, the prophet said, "Source is wrong. This, like the larger beasts you saw today, is simply a figure that Ma pleases to inhabit. Always feline. She does not usually like guests."

"She likes *me*," Xar declared proudly. "Gods love me."

With Lucille interpreting constantly at her side, U6-93 walked over to pet the cat. She was smiling painted teeth. "See? What did I tell you. Such a thing has never happened before in my life nor any of which I have heard. Ma is in part a huntergod. She does not like competition but senses not such a thing in the Apechi spirit."

"Does this give us any clues as to the nature of the Apechi deity?" Ming asked.

"It gives us more mysteries, but all of them pleasant. If I were to guess, which I should not but shall anyway because my curiosity is so piqued as to be like a spring irrepressible, I would hazard two theories. One, I see this Apechi creature as a being of constant motion. Always moving, always seeming to change. It could well be that Ma is fascinated in much the same way as she is by our armor and in fact even more so because this motion exists on the conjectural plane. Two, I see this Apechi creature is in the habit of infecting human beings. Xar is himself inhabited. Perhaps the same power which grants it this possessive skill grants it human knowledge, your perception, your reason. It does seem to me like your god has a notion of self-control. This is highly irregular. Gods do not have motives as such; they do not work in a way such as we mortal beings can properly perceive and so I must be wrong." She waited for Lucille to finish and then added, "The Red steward carries the Apechi god, too."

Ming flushed—furious, jealous.

Xar laughed. "What?"

"I have told you but I will repeat it if that is your desire. The Red steward is possessed. I see it clearly. My cardinals have cautioned me as is their responsibility to be careful with our budding relationship, but I admit myself quite taken with longing to know of what this thing of yours is made. To see allies both concrete and metaphysical on the Crysthian thrones . . . well. What a world that would be."

Thirsty for the blood of his former masters, Lucille hissed, "Yes."

The prophet laughed a low, happy delight at her pet traitor before turning to Ming, "Your agitation is infecting my cardinals."

"I apologize," she answered. "But perhaps it should. We must act."

"Do not presume to tell Her Holiness what she should do. You never even graduated, you never rose high enough to lose your hands," Lucille.

Xar tensed. Ma's vehicle raised its head, disturbed by his movement. The stars above reflected in the depth of its eyes. Abyss, abyss. Silence.

"I see." Ming spoke into the quiet, her voice soft. "It isn't a hum. It's a purr, isn't it? The planet purrs."

"Yes, I suppose," Lucille said. "If you want to put it like that."

"I do." Ming's voice still laxly veiling their argument to those without the language to hear beyond her tone. "And you will not use me as an outlet for your frustration with yourself, Lucille. You let them take your hands, I will keep mine and take their thrones. I did not graduate because I was busy assassinating an emperor. You know that. You should also know that envy is a bad look on a man already a traitor."

"If I am a traitor, what are you?"

"Conqueror," she said, as if it were the punch line to a clever joke.

Ma's tail began to twitch. Xar said, "Ow."

"Best not to stop petting her," advised a cardinal.

Lucille went back to translating, opting to pretend he hadn't been made to look like a bitch.

"This is the consecrated thread you brought?" U6-93 asked.

Ming nodded confirmation.

U6-93 lifted the strand from the table with a deferential thumb and forefinger. Inspecting it, she spoke and Lucille said, "She doesn't think that this will work."

"It did last time we had a . . . god knower," Xar said.

Xar and Ming had summoned their god's power before, long ago, with the guidance of the only Apechi priest. They had tried again since his death. Much blood, no avail.

The batcardinal raised his fingers for a turn with the Apechi holy object. He touched it with his tongue. He spoke and Lucille said, "When you achieved this last, you had with you the guidance of one who knew well the god itself. This may be the best course of manipulation but not for being known."

"What does that mean?" Xar asked.

Lucille shrugged. "No idea. He speaks even worse than Dash, I never know what he's talking about."

"I think he means that the Apechi priest knew what he was doing, but they don't," Ming offered. "But we were there—we did it. Stitching two infected together just like this."

U6-93 said something decisive which made the cardinals retreat to places at the room's outer circle, standing over runes carved into the tile. Ma does not care about runes, the purpose of ritual is to concentrate human minds.

"Should we move?" Xar asked.

"We'll be fine," Lucille said. "They're operating elsewhere. You know"—he waved his metal forearms around mysteriously and repeated—"elsewhere."

The cardinals began to whisper. U6-93 took a scalpel, said a prayer to herself. She did not know what she was doing, but she was trying anyway, pushing Ma into the joined bodies and trying to pull the Apechi deity from them.

Ma's puppet hopped from Xar's lap, tail a hook of gray fur. She couldn't get purchase on the tile to leap. Lucille rushed to pick her up and placed her onto the table where she lapped purring at the blood that flowed. The room quivered with her delight.

U6-93 went still, her hands frozen in place, needle pointing upward at the stars. She had been stitching the two bodies together by the arm, wounding them into one as the Apechi priest had done. Her jaw moved. The cardinals, eyes closed, must have perceived whatever energy held their prophet paralyzed for they had stopped their whispering.

Something joined Ma's purr. Something electrical in tone, a buzzing unease which grated where Ma soothed. Lucille looked to Xar and whispered, "Is this yours?"

Xar nodded. Ming was completely still, afraid to move, as if she in her animal irrelevance might disturb the communion of ghosts. She hadn't felt the thunderous whine of the Apechi god since the uprising on Apech, since it had consumed the one man she thought capable of controlling it.

One of the drugged bodies stirred, shards of bone nuzzling beneath its skin at the joints, growing longer, subsuming its face in a thatch of osteotopography. They could all hear it, the expansion of bone. The noise of deformity ticked wetly as it broke the skin.

Xar stood, approached the statue figure of U6-93. He leaned toward her to listen then said: "She's speaking Apechi."

"I hear it." Ming.

A crack as the deforming body failed, chest caving in on itself with the weight of its tumored ribs.

Xar switched to his native tongue, "Can you hear us?"

Deadly stasis but for her jaw and her tongue, the prophet muttered. Mutter. Mutter.

The batcardinal's voice from the perimeter of the room, "It's *talking* through her? No. We are not prepared for this."

He stepped forward. Ma's creature growled but did not look up from her lickings and so he did not break his stride. He came to his prophet and removed the thread from her hands, squeezed her arms to bring her back.

The other cardinals came forward after him. Examining the spent body, picking at the bone. The other was still alive.

"Why did you stop? Is that it?!" Ming, enraged.

"What were you expecting?" Lucille, smug. "We have to manufacture all that spectacle at the stadium ourselves, deities don't care much for our entertainment."

"I don't care to be entertained, you fucking imbecile, I care to be informed."

U6-93 wheezed, coming back into the room, surfacing from the nowhere. She turned to Xar and Ming, hands raised in request for their focus. She babbled nonsense at them. She tried again. Seeing no recognition in their faces she snarled in frustration and kept going, more babble sound. Trying to form alien words which she had heard in the dark.

"Sccg," she said. "Brrrrg masccgds"

"Oh dear." Lucille.

Xar whispering to himself in Apechi, focusing on the prophet's mouth, trying to find the sound. "*Bring me*?" he suggested.

Her eyes lit up. She pointed at his face, not wanting to stop her repetition nor hear anything that might dispel the trace of foreign language in her mind.

"Bring me scccgds. Bring me . . . Bring me . . ."

"Stewards," Xar said, and the prophet fell quiet.

Xar turned to Ming, repeated in Apechi, "Bring me the stewards."

"What do they mean, these words I've been compelled to say?" asked the prophet.

"What?" translated Lucille.

They told her. A cardinal helped her into a chair.

"It didn't want them." she said, indicating the Apechi bodies. "A god. Such a thing should not be able to talk. Such a thing should not be able to . . . want. It spoke to me. Something spoke to me. In your language, not Crysthian? Oh. This is wrong."

"It wants us to try this ritual again with the stewards?" Ming inquired, her hopes rising.

"Impossible," she answered.

"Xar!" Ming rounded on him.

"What? What do you want me to do? It's not my fault."

"Something," said U6-93, "is going on here. Something . . . uneldritch."

The batcardinal put his hand to his face, another gasped.

"Lucille for fuck's sake what is she saying?" Ming shouted.

"Uh, something weird is happening."

"No shit."

"You will stop your arguing with them, blackhand. I don't know what you're saying but I hear your tone," batcardinal barked at Lucille, "You can be replaced here."

Made bitch twofold, Lucille sulked.

They all waited, watching the lines across U6-93's face as she thought, eyes closed. Finally she said, "There are things at play here which I do not and cannot for now understand. I need to know. I believe this is not merely curiosity but imperative. Our great rival has been taken hold of by this thing you have brought upon them. I am uncertain, I am concerned. But I am only human—I cannot see far into the world where these things of which I am uncertain are happening. Ma can, and Ma in her fickle might is not afraid. Who are the stewards and how do we fetch them here?"

22

U6-93 watched her favorite cardinal. His eyes flickered beneath their lids. She was an intruder, though she did not feel the part. He was deep in communion. His concentration was so deep in fact that he had forgotten the time. Regardless, she did not wake him. It was rare that she could steal an opportunity to observe her highest court at their worship.

She had hoped he would be here when she hadn't found him in his lobby. They were to meet Crysth's representatives once again in a more intimate setting—the obsidian stalagmite in which the batcardinal lived. It was as distinctive a building as his suit. Rivers of green algae ran over the stone, shaped into ever-changing suggestions of movement like the unfurling of wings. No bats could live in the wild—too squeaky and exciting, they had been batted from the sky by the god's eviscerating curiosity. But they lived here, tended and caged. He wore the animals like a cilice, part of him always focused on keeping Ma from striking them down.

The clicking patter of clawed feet outside told U6-93 that the cardinal was on his way back to his body. She stood to close the door. He would be able to reach the handle on the cat's hind legs, it would be good for him to practice its dexterity.

A minute of fumbling later and the front half of a big cat thudded into the room, complaining. Antenna tufts of fur grew from the tops of its ears and the prophet twirled one of these around her finger as it rubbed against her legs. On the bed, the cardinal twitched, trying to wake himself, trying to lurch out of the paralysis he had lulled himself carefully beyond.

"Fivepoint." She snapped his name. Her tone was unpleasant but the intention was friendly, helping him find his way back.

He groaned a little as he opened his eyes. The movement seemed painful, hard won.

Ma's deipuppet flopped, a normal cat once again, bored to find itself in a bedroom.

"Late," he said, struggling upright. "I'm late?"

Her silence confirmed it. Mind returning, he reached for a cup at his bedside and sipped.

"The time is not a matter for concern. You are not in the habit of keeping me waiting and I am glad to see you practice, you will have to restrain Ma while we attack the Zetland, if it comes to that," she said.

"Alone?"

"No. We will need everyone, even those newly initiated. War on her own planet. So much frenzy, so much bloodshed. She will be uncontrollable if she is allowed to see it. We cannot let her see it."

Despite his love for Ma he winced at the thought. And it was love—the passionate, zealous love that comes with purposefully navigating beyond the knowledge that its object is harmful. Ma could be gentle, but never kind.

U6-93 approached him as he dressed, winding a translator over his ear.

"Lucille?" he asked.

"I have told him to stay away. I have done so as a show of earnestness. I wish Crysth not to be offended. I wish to give them a chance." She felt him inhale to speak, then change his mind. "You were going to say something. Do so or I will be unable to stop myself from inventing my own criticisms and placing them in your mouth without your consent."

"I am as surprised as Lucille by your fondness for Crysth."

"I see." She finished fiddling with his translator then swept her beads away to show him her own. "It is not fondness, as I have already said.

Although I confess that it is nostalgia. Avon Stal has been important to me. Her existence, her animosity, and yes her affection have helped me to situate myself. She is all that remains of the world I knew before we turned Ma into what it is now. I do not want to lose her. I like even now to see her ship hovering above the Zetland. I find it comforting. I find her comforting."

"Disgusting."

She smiled, agreeing. "Thankfully for me, the course which leads to her preservation is also the most practical in this instance. The Apechi command want thrones, not heads. It is in their interest and therefore ours to make the transition as bloodless as possible. The people common of Crysth may never care nor notice that we have switched their leadership. The empire of Ma-Crysth. It even sounds beautiful. All that power, all those things, nothing in our way."

"What things?"

"Do you not remember Muhr wine? It flowed plenty here before all the embargoes they insist upon us. You must have been born too late. A deliciousness the likes of which I have never tasted again."

His spiked teeth shone in silver devilgrin as he said, "May we tell history that we overthrew Crysth for the sake of wine? It's as good a reason as any."

*

Avon Stal and Rhododendron looked an odd pair. U6-93 liked that about Crysth—there was no uniformity among them even though they had uniforms. But she liked it in the way that an adult likes animation designed for children, a momentary delight followed by a sensation of being aesthetically overwhelmed. Too garish, too silly. Lights span and flashed on the emperor's torso, blue silk flowed in strips around Avon's waist.

"Good afternoon," said Rhododendron, raising his palm in the Ma wave. "Thank you for inviting us to your home."

"I see you left the 'ambassador' Lucille wherever you keep him. A cage I hope," Avon said.

The prophet spoke into the translator, which said, "It is a cage he believes he fled. But yes, today it will be we four alone. I have accepted the discomfort of this machine as a show of friendliness to you, I assumed it would be understood as such."

"It is." Rhododendron, quickly. "Please do not mistake our hatred of Lucille as a distaste for you."

"We do no such thing and there is no need to," said the batcardinal. "Your existence declares its hatred for us in every action, we have no desire to pretend otherwise."

Avon bowed a little. "Agreed. Shall we walk? I know you keep some of those marvelous big cats out here, I heard one on the way in."

"You will see it." The prophet gestured forward and they followed, walking together along the cardinal's garden path. "That is why we brought you here."

Harried-looking priests zigzagged over the grounds, disappearing and reappearing, brooms and books and hedge trimmers in hand. Ma's priests feared the cardinals, even though its civilians did not. The priests had a clearer idea of how much power the higher clergy controlled. To denaturalize the deity was to live in constant fear, realizing always that their world was held together by human concentration. Once you had seen it, Ma's capital shifted from city to submarine; an object constantly vulnerable to the enormous, unthinking monstrosity that supported it.

The four of them came to a new part of the garden. A small obstacle course, a few training dummies. A recess containing a heap of sleeping animal.

"Oh my go—sorry. Fuck." said Avon when they saw it.

U6-93 grinned. "Beautiful, isn't he?"

Rhododendron leaned over the railing, looking into the pit, his bioware ticking on his arms. "What is it?"

"The residents of the planet from which we took him called the species *hannefor*."

The emperor's lip curled. "Called? Is the past tense a quirk of the translator or are there none of these people left to speak?"

Silver teeth leered their response.

"And you can possess these *hannefor* with Ma?" Avon said. "I cannot tell whether this thing is feline or reptile."

"Ma recognizes it." The prophet's true voice was a whisper beneath the translator's flat growl.

Down in the pit, gray skin showed where its ribs distended the animal's thin pelt. Its claws were long, curved, retractable into huge paws. But its most remarkable feature save its size was its face. Small ears and front set eyes on a round head which elongated into a pointed mouth, slit nostrils, a mess of teeth. The fangs parted slightly as it dreamed.

"I see excess skin around the leg joints. Tell me it doesn't fly," said Avon.

"Not quite. It glides. It is a forest creature." U6-93, delighted by Avon's recognition of the creature's utility. "It hunts in packs to find its way into villages undetected. It is a dangerous thing. There are very many of them."

"You are showing us a weapon." Rhododendron turned his back to it. "Are we to read this as a threat?"

"The opposite," said the batcardinal. "We are showing our hand, our newest military development. We are letting you in on a state secret."

"Can we see you controlling it?" Avon asked.

"You're seeing that right now. It isn't tethered." The batcardinal let out a derisive laugh as Rhododendron flinched away from the railing.

"We come to you in a moment of weakness and you show us strength. It is difficult to interpret this as a gesture of friendship." Avon said.

"Our gestures can be misread, sometimes simply wrong. We are alien, after all." U6-93, being genuine.

"And you want our help. Does it not reassure you to see that you come for competent aid?"

Relenting a little, Rhododendron said, "So you will help us?"

"I will commune with the Apechi deity. I will find out what it is, seek a way to control it."

Avon sighed. "May we ask what you are expecting in return?"

"No payment in the traditional sense," the prophet answered. "It is in our interest to find out what this new and very powerful deity is made of. But we will need a show of faith, from the faithless."

"Go on." Rhododendron.

"Your stewards will remain with us throughout our dealings with this deity."

Both Crysthian expressions morphed into confusion.

Avon said, "You want to hold Ella and Speaker hostage? Ella and Speaker?"

"What the hell for?" Rhododendron, amazed.

"I would pay you to take them." Avon, equally so.

U6-93 kept herself carefully serene. "It is only the pair?"

"Yes," Rhododendron said. "Why do you want them? Is this hostages we are talking about?"

Silence.

"I see," said Avon. "You didn't ask me for a hostage last time, Dash."

Rhododendron glanced at her, said: "Ah."

"Last time I was just exorcising a few of those sad demon creatures you keep as slaves in the machines. A god is far greater a task."

"Which is exactly why it makes no sense that you would not extract a prize," Avon accused.

"The prize will be stability."

"I am going to ask a yes or no question," Rhododendron said. "Do you intend to harm our stewards?"

Silence.

"Answer the question."

The lights on Rhododendron's chest flared.

"No?" tried the cardinal.

"What?! You know that I know when you are lying. My sensors cannot be mistaken. How dare you?"

"Why? What do you want to do with them? This is absurd." Avon, outraged.

"It does not matter. I will not hear further. I will not be lied to," Rhododendron thundered.

Avon seemed genuinely hurt. "What do you want to do with them?"

"Perhaps this bioware of yours is less effective on foreign—" began Fivepoint.

"Stop it. No lies. They know us now," said the prophet. Turning to Rhododendron she said, "Ma will be pleased."

"You were going to sacrifice my actual twin to your god? You space-freak minded creeps, what is wrong with you?"

"I thought this was going so well," Avon mused.

"Think about it," said the batcardinal. "Isn't it in your interest to make sacrifices, materialist? Is two not fewer than the rest of you?"

"Is this just some rancid display of dominance?" Rhododendron, almost spitting. "Like showing us this—this devil flying squirrel?"

"*Squirrel*," repeated the prophet. "I like that word. *Squirrel*. Far better than *hannefor*."

"You people are mad."

"Rhododendron, please," Avon begged. "We can work with this."

"Like fuck we can."

The general made apologetic eye contact with the prophet before she followed in the wake of Rhododendron's long-legged storming from the garden.

"Ah well," breathed the batcardinal. "We tried."

"We should not have lied. I was wrong. I did this wrongly. If I had said it plain then perhaps he could have seen the deal as pure mathematics. I have doomed them myself."

Her cardinal shrugged. "Alas. So are we calling it squirrel now?"

23

Night sparkled over Ma's capital city, its architecture writhing with bioluminescent sludge. At its center, the cathedral lunged skyward like a giant sundial over districts of jagged rock. Ming's hands grasped a railing on its roof, staring into the distance where she knew the Zetland lay—its position marked by Avon Stal's warmachine floating protectively above.

"Ready?" asked Xar.

She nodded.

Behind them Lucille said, "Do not take Ella lightly, he acts a jester but he is war—only vanity will keep him unprepared. Speaker is useless but will have a seeking knife. Rhododendron is not battle-designed but still very strong. If you even *see* Vard or any of the Stals you are dead. Run the moment you suspect their approach."

"Would it make you feel better if we wrote that on our arms? How many times now?" Ming.

"Please, please do not fail." Lucille.

"We won't. We can't." Xar.

"Avon is on her ship. Vard is incapacitated somehow." Ming.

"I don't trust it. Fear them."

"We're going to 'fuck them up.'" Xar, who had been trying to colloquialize his Crysthian.

"Absolutely no fucking up. Just slip in there, secure the stewards-"

"And consolidate power from the inside," they chorused.

"We know!" Xar.

"Your role in this has ended already, Lucille. Allow us to focus." Ming.

"We will be back with those stewards or not at all, either way you win. Unless you would miss us?"

"Absolutely not."

"Well then, go the fuck to bed while we do our job." Xar.

"You should show me some respect, do you think those maps of the Zetland just materialized out of nowhere?! And I want that keychip back when you're done thank you very much."

"Piss off." Xar.

As Lucille pissed off, Ming said, "Treacherous little shit."

"None treacherous or shittier. Come on, my team is ready."

She followed him to one of the impossible vehicles piloted by Ma's cardinals. Apechi soldiers prattled excitedly around it—undisciplined but strong with the undecipherable power the deity pumps into them. A few separated from the main group to flank Ming when they saw her.

"I can take you to your entrance but no farther." rumbled a cardinal's translator. "We are all needed to hold Ma away."

"Where's bat?" Xar.

With a smirk the cardinal answered, "5.862 will be in command up here when we begin, but he is with Squirrel on the ground right now. Another car will take you and your guards to him." This last to Ming.

"Now?" Ming.

No answer. The cardinal looked away to give Ming and Xar a moment together that they did not need. They did not say goodbye, they did not say good luck. The god of Apech had shown Xar that they would win. He knew it could lie, but never yet to him.

Ming stepped out of the ship and into the batcardinal's attention. He nodded to her, as did Squirrel. The gesture made Ming realize that the creature was, at that moment, the prophet. The cardinal laughed at her expression of surprise.

"Uncanny?" he asked through the translator.

"More so than I expected. I have seen this kind of thing before but not so well controlled, not so human. Certainly never so impressive an animal."

Squirrel clacked its alligator mouth, another communication from U6-93.

"Our prophet is the best. Ma is very powerful."

"And yet you're certain you can hold her back? If she senses—"

"I do not need you to tell me what will happen if Ma gets excited. That is not your concern and your concern it shall never be. Go with Squirrel, go in command of your damaged gods."

Ming bowed in apology. She straightened her suit as she rose again—maroon robe with a leather torso which would mark her as a high ranking Red to anybody in the Zetland with the knowledge to read it. Armor beneath, which would be unnecessary if all went according to plan. She was to slither into the Red wing in the confusion of the onslaught, use the key scraped from Lucille's old prosthetics to seal she and her guards into the control room. Cuckoos under the cover of chaos.

A bishop came forward, wiry and bruised in a symmetrical, linear fashion. She held a harness which was shaped just like her injuries.

"It will hurt," she said in Crysthian, fastening the thing around Ming's torso. "You must make effort to control muscles, remain even. Long climb." She stepped back to weigh up Ming's guards and directed them to certain hooks on Squirrel's own harness. They patted its fur, excited and unafraid.

Ming glanced again to where she knew the Zetland must be. They felt so secure with Avon Stal's warship above them that they had opened some of the space-shutters, leaving entrances vulnerable. Still, the technomancers would be able to sense an unwanted presence the moment it touched the ship. The ship was made of them, they were made of it.

Squirrel smelled like pond. Its skin tugged the fabric of Ming's suit. She held on to the handles at its shoulder blade, checked the Apechi warriors around her. They were delighted by the task of protecting her, if somewhat disappointed to be left out of the main assault. This was important. And they got to ride Squirrel.

"Muscles tense," commanded the bishop, watching them adjust.

The batcardinal came over to check their attachments. He spoke to Squirrel as he did. U6-93 cracked responses with its teeth.

"You may be waiting some time for my signal," he said to Ming. "Do not panic, do not attempt to dismount. U6-93 is in command until the moment you are in the palace."

"Your Holiness." The cavalry bishop held her hand up in the motion that said she was reading a text message. "The defeated gods are amassing. The archbishops are holding them in R4. They are ready for you to begin."

He smiled his fanged pleasure and turned to Ming. "I will see you again."

The smile solidified on his face as he turned. A gleam may have faded from his silver eyes, but they were silver so that wasn't possible. He was annoyed, nagged by a certainty that he should refuse his orders while unable to think of an alternative plan. It would not be his first rebellion. Decision-making on Ma was not unilateral; U6-93 was their vector between god and man but they all knew this did not make her omnipotent in political matters. She and her cardinals could argue for days.

He climbed into his car, waved his hand in an irritated fashion for someone else to pilot it. Someone did, incompetently. Fivepoint allowed the jolting to go on for around a minute before taking over, effortlessly snatching Ma's invisible reins with such force that the unfortunate man lost consciousness. The others, who had been sitting in silence, fell quieter.

His personal clergy were already at work by the time he arrived. They were borrowing another cardinal's astronomy tower—which also bothered him—but it happened to have a direct view of Avon's ship.

He stared at the ship. Accursed sinister orb. Even from this distance he could make out the lights of activity within its opaque outer shell. It was designed never to land, he knew. This also annoyed him—the pure, shameless arrogance of it. He wanted to smash it out of the sky, crush it.

Hear them scream. Make that rude little general watch what he did to them. He felt a twitch in his cock and looked away, focusing instead on the lines being daubed onto the floor.

He was keeping Ma's attention away from the room and the god was getting upset. His servants could feel her, coiling tight energy. They were afraid and in their fear they were making mistakes. The cardinal's feet appeared in their line of sight as they worked. They would apologize, shrink, assure him that they were fixing it. Listen terrified as his soft footsteps receded to haunt another.

This is his main dissimilarity from U6-93, as far as the worship of Ma is concerned. He is a perfectionist. He plays instruments, he cooks and he tinkers. It had been he who first suggested the use of runes, symbols and patterns to help the clergy to focus entirely on Ma. He created a new alphabet, which he demanded everybody take extremely seriously and which everybody did because it worked. Unlike U6-93 who could somehow see the deities as clearly as if they lived in the real, breathing world, he and the others needed help. Something to trick their minds, self-hypnosis. Candles, holy water, glowing paint. They did not let anybody in on the secret of the charade until the highest ranks—although to reach them you had to have already figured it out for yourself. The cardinals maintained pretense at times such as these not because they feared public opinion if the runes were discovered to be manmade, but because the pretense helped them to pretend. Right then, the batcardinal was convinced that his own alphabet was sacred. That is what made it so.

Stupid orb. He allowed himself to look at the ship again. Destroying it completely would be certain death for everyone in the capital. Perhaps the planet. He would be grinning in satisfied spite as the nuclear flames consumed him but he really better not.

He allowed a little of Ma's power to fuss around him, relieving some tension in the room. The god's tone shifted from a whine to the excited rumble of distant thunder.

"Just hit Avon Stal's ship," U6-93 had told him. "Once, a warning shot to scare her off." The prophet had said that Avon Stal is not stupid, that she has been here before. She knows how strong Ma is. She will not risk her ship for the sake of a dying palace. She will flee. Things of this nature.

As far as he was concerned, the prophet was putting them all at risk for the sake of what she plainly admitted was her own sentimentality.

But he could not think of an alternative. The prophet had arrived at the only viable battle plan via the most disingenuous route—her desire to see Avon Stal survive. The sheer illogicality of it was deeply upsetting to him.

His anger would be useful. He stood in the center of the room, touched a hand to his chest, where it activated the unfurling of his perfect silver wings. Another trick, the distribution of their weight, helped him to concentrate, as did the satisfaction at having so perfectly designed them.

He endeavored to make eye contact with the orb. Fuck you, orb.

The challenge was to hold Ma back while using her to lash out at the same time. It would require the attention of everyone not engaged in shepherding the halfgods toward the Zetland. Godherding, fortunately, was not a difficult task. The Zetland was a hive of virgin human beings, untouched by another deity. It was practically magnetized, a hull full of raw material for deistic expansion; uncaged, the weakened monsters would crawl toward it whether Ma's priests nipped at their heels or not.

Runes shone underfoot. He was ready.

*

Squirrel's puppetmaster had known that the blast was coming. The animal crouched low to the ground, ears back.

"Put your damn heads down," snapped Ming in Apechi. Her soldiers thought that they were invulnerable. Their god had filled them with its notion of irrevocable certainty, which Ming quietly distrusted because she knew that this is exactly what she would do to them if she had the ability herself.

A rush of air. A silence. The sphere moved. And then they heard it.

*

The floating ruins in the Zetland's palace gardens did not twitch, but the room shook around them. A rumble from above, glass shaking in its frame. Technomancers screaming, hands clawing at the ringing metal in their skulls. U6-93's crusaders hadn't predicted this, but it will be the shock of the unreal boom which prevents the techs from closing the Zetland's doors before the invaders have time to use them.

Ella's bedroom window rippled. He watched it with a dazed inevitability, surprised only that it was happening so soon.

*

Batcardinal's clergy cheered, standing to applaud the perfect precision it had taken for him to reach out, grab Avon's ship, and push it. No damage, just a warning, just as he had been told.

Sweat dripped into his eyes. Someone ran forward with a cold cloth. He couldn't hear the celebration. He was trying not to vomit.

The force of the ship's movement hit them, rumbling into the tower. Something else they had not predicted. He fell. The glass window shattered, tearing through the clergy's faces and hands. They felt Ma rise. Blood, energy, movement. All bringing her dreadful curiosity to the surface. They ignored their wounds and even batcardinal in his sickened daze began to pull her back, luring her down away from the world.

He struggled to his front, lifted his head to watch Avon's ship, allowed himself to throw up and felt worse. The ship was patterned with circles of roving light. He fought to his knees and stared in petrified disbelief as the sphere began to come apart. Globules of tiny drones detaching from the main throng of its crust and forming rings in the sky. Spinning flocks with components so small they looked like liquid. Avon wasn't going to flee, she was fighting back.

*

Ella hammered his fists against the window, yelling encouragement at the flow of spinning death overhead.

24

Batcardinal heaved himself from the floor, palms slit and bleeding. Avon's two symmetrical dronecircles grew brighter as they span, white verging on blue. His eyes ached. He looked away but the spectacle advanced in the shattered reflection of bloody glass beneath him. He whispered to himself, to his god. Mostly to himself.

He staggered upright. Wings broken, weight unfamiliar. Used the momentum of his body to force his mind back into the sticky, unconscious depths where Ma's power lay.

He lashed out with Ma once more. Then he threw up again and fell, blacked out.

What he had meant to do was to destroy Avon's machines entirely, what he had achieved was to fire another boom of pressure into one of the dronecircles. His second attack was almost as harmless as his first. The circle went dull, splitting, millions of nanobots falling from the sky. More zipping confused back into their flock.

*

Avon Stal's body was submerged, plugged into the center of the sphere. Her own metal trance, her own form of worship.

It was the batcardinal's second, failed attack which made her realize that they were not threatening her warship. His mistake showed her that she was not under attack, she was being invited to run. Her orders charged along the ship's wires to her captains. *Pull back. We are leaving.* Their disgust raced back to her—complaints, confusion.

This is why she detached her ship from the grid. Without the supremacy of the Zetland technomancers she has speed and freedom. She communicates with her captains instantly. Her body is the machine. One animal, feeling through space. She conceals nothing when she sends her thoughts to them, packaging her entire emotional manifesto in electrical signals which show them her intent.

We must abandon the Zetland. Ma was its only hope. The prophet is inviting us to save ourselves, and she is right. The Crysthian alliance has already split. Vard is dead, Ella is under arrest. Juniper and Cull are dead. Daksha is gone. We are all that is left of Military. We can die with Rhododendron or we can retreat, wait, then return to negotiate with the inevitable new order.

The message that came back to her, carried across the cables of her expanded consciousness, was a wail. A collective sob, mourning. But the delicate perfection of the machine showed her that it was not entirely the Zetland's loss which caused their anguish—they pitied themselves for having lived to see the end. They were with her.

She rewarded them by allowing herself a moment's pettiness. She smiled through the trance as she took control of a dronecircle, her fingers twitched.

*

Xar Kis stood at the rear of the vanguard of ruined gods, arms behind his back. Waiting patiently for the situation with the drones to resolve itself. He wasn't worried about the behavior of any orb, nuclear or otherwise. He knew he was going to win.

This is why, when Avon's spiral vortex combusted into a laser of white doom in the direction of Ma's cathedral, he laughed.

It was an architectural circumcision. The slanted stone pyramid severed in a perfect line, sliding slowly onto the surrounding buildings.

Silent but for the chuckle in Xar's throat the soldiers watched, stared amazed at the spherical ship as it ascended. The zapping of the cathedral's roof seemed its only intent; casual harm done, it was leaving.

"What the hell was that?" asked one of Xar's soldiers.

"I think Avon Stal said, *fuck you*," he replied. "And I also think that was our cue to advance."

25

A tech staggered through the Zetland's intestinal walls, bouncing off corners onto the racing streams that would take her back to her sector. The ship's pulse thudded. Holding her jaw, the sound of Ma's first attack still itching in her brain, every one of the palace's complaints was an agony in her metal face. Without a ring of deimancers to protect them, Ma's boom of unreal energy had set the techs' hypersensitive alterations screaming. Others rushing past, every direction. All alarms blaring. Unidentifiable things at a dozen different doors. Her part of the machine calling out to her with a sad bleating in her skull.

She burst out of the wall to see the problem. Nothing became clearer.

The spacedoor was trying to close. It rattled as it did so, thrashing against the strength of whatever inimical thing held it back.

Military uniforms yelling at one another. An array of weapons. A spattering of Greens and maroon-colored Reds trying to help, making it worse. The tech pushed her way to the front of the crowd, making herself known and commanding their attention by shutting off the alarm.

"We can't shoot it," called a Military captain, automatically placing the technomancer in charge—this was Zetland business. "The bullets might shatter the window. We've tried lasers and as much heat and cold as we dare."

"Can you cut it?" She winced as she spoke, every movement set her bioware ringing again.

"We just sent someone for a ladder. They're . . . there."

The ladder's fetcher set it gently against the glass. A few feet from its top was the thing, the door trying to close around it.

The thing seemed like no thing at all. Like a stain, textured. A patch of moss bleeding through the glass. Only the Zetland's complaints betrayed it for an object so strong as to be unnatural.

"Stay away from it, try a spear!" someone said.

"Should we try throwing stuff?" someone else.

"Nobody throw anything!" the tech.

The Military captain said, "Spear's a good idea, did anyone bring a spear?"

Of course, someone had. Crysth's Military instinctively run into battle with as vast an array of weapons they can carry; space exploration teaches you not to make assumptions about vulnerability. A cheer as someone handed one over. Cries of encouragement to be careful.

The moss-thing appeared to be growing.

As he neared the ladder's apex the bespeared man slowed, called back to the crowd: "It looks like . . . coral."

Varying noises replied, all seemed to agree that this was alarming despite the complete and utter absence of anything that could be said to the inverse effect.

"I can hear the sea," he added, distantly.

"Don't listen to the fucker."

"Spear it!"

The rear doors crashed open, another crowd thronging in to join them, also yelling.

"Run! Run!" said the new crowd.

"What are you running from?"

"Run!"

Those in blue grabbed their weapons, hustled to the edge as others fled from the side door, joining the screaming crowd. Some of the newcomers stayed to help, receiving pistols and swords, bows and seeking knives, others taking plastic devices which shot only light.

"What is it?"

"Don't know."

"It's orange!" This was sobbed.

The technomancer's metal face spoke to her. *Dozens of ruptures, unnatural forces inside the Zetland. More coming. Soldiers on the ground. Fight. Clear the exterior so that we can get airborne.*

"No retreat!" she screamed. "Orders received. No retreat!"

The thing emerged. Orange it was. Hexagonal, also. It drifted soundlessly, slowly toward them. A pace gentler than a walk.

People started to throw, to fire. Knives clattered to the ground, arrows fell, soft bullets ricocheted. But the most distressing thing was that each object, having failed in its onslaught, collapsed newly orange.

"What the fuck!"

"It just turns things orange?"

"No! No, don't touch it, it's killing people!"

"What do they die of?"

"We don't know!"

The hexagon kept coming. The crowd thinned around it, forming a circle. Someone with a sword dashed forward to stab at it, found it rock hard and glass smooth, dropped their oranged weapon in terror.

Behind them, the ladder fell. The man who had been standing on it did not. He floated ten feet above them, still facing the coral invader.

"Sir, get down!"

The floating man did not respond.

"Okay, okay, we're gonna seal it in this room," called a higher-ranking Military. "Everybody ready to run?"

"Our orders are no retreat!"

"Are you not seeing this thing? What do you want us to do?"

"We can't leave the captain—look, the coral thing's got him!"

They looked. In the moment of their distraction the hexagon tilted and lurched forward, hungry, desperate, touching a group of three with its angles.

Nobody had expected it could move so quickly. They flattened back, watching those it had touched.

Orange. Their skin was orange, their clothes were orange. Their hair, orange.

They screamed, holding up their orange hands, looking around with pupilless orange eyes. One began to clutch at her throat. Orange fingers orange neck and as she opened her mouth they saw the orange teeth, the orange tongue.

The orange people fell to the ground. Their screams were brief, high and repetitive as if in horror rather than pain—until they were quiet. Their bodies curled up hard like dead, orange spiders.

Everyone ran. The floating man remained.

*

"It's going to break through."

"Shh."

A tech knelt at the bottom of the door, eyes closed, communicating with the Zetland.

Thud. Thud.

They didn't know yet what thudded outside, but they knew that it had teeth. They had glimpsed the fangs through a tiny portal window nobody now dared approach. Guns focused on the glass, watching the technomancer. Hoping for a miracle.

Red light flashed from outside, the Zetland's defense system activated. Everything went still, the thudding stopped.

An intake of breath from the soldiers, wondering if they dared believe that it was over.

Screams were heard from elsewhere in the ship. Sirens.

"I think I lasered it?" suggested the tech, turning to the mob.

The thing outside disagreed. The door boomed inward, flattening the tech. A scent of burnt fur and flesh. Soldiers opening fire.

The laser had only annoyed the beast. Its snout emerged, wolflike—bigger.

It withdrew its head from the door and tried to squeeze its body through. Too small, too big. It started thrashing itself against the wall again. The machine was falling apart. Their bullets seemed irrelevant. This is not a fortress it is a palace and the creature will get inside.

When get inside it did, they saw its torso had been severed at the waist but that the creature did not care. Trailing gore and shit, it dragged itself snapping through the ruin. Apelike arms battering into the soldiers, a man caught at the end of a long-hooked claw and flailed ragdoll through his comrades as the godhand kept swiping at them indiscriminately.

Laser-fire concentrated on its eyes, and a melting white goo slopped from sockets the size of a human head, but the creature didn't need sight. There was so much blood on the Zetland's polished floors that those with edged weapons could barely steady themselves to strike, but they hacked off its two remaining limbs as the head continued to bite. Automatic weapons fired into the muzzle until its snout was blunt gristle on a destroyed face.

There was no celebration when its chest stopped heaving. Too much destruction, too many gone. Dragging the injured out of the carnage. Listening to the sobs of those the dead left behind.

Standing outside looking down at the creature's severed legs, Xar Kis said: "Ghastly."

"I can't believe they killed that thing," observed one of his lieutenants, genuinely impressed.

"Mm. Very inspiring. Get in there and clear the way."

A gesture to the rest of the squadron and the Apechi soldiers were swarming inside, clambering over the inanimate hunk of flesh which almost blocked their way.

Apech's fighters had not yet bothered with guns, nor really had any to try. They fought with the power of a god that could see through time and tell them what to do. They knew exactly how to move. When they were lucky their bodies got out of the way of the bullets that raced toward them, when they were unlucky they put it down to god's will. They moved, sometimes in stop-motion, channeling strength from other versions of themselves even though they had no idea that's what they were doing. But they were relatively few. If the Crysthian soldiers weren't so afraid, disorganized, fraught, then Apech would surely lose.

Godmagic surged over the wolf's corpse. The battered soldiers inside the Zetland barely had time to aim. Apech tore through them.

*

Rhododendron had watched the retreat of Avon's ship without comment. In the safety of his thoughts, he decided that this must have been her plan all along. Abandonment. His bioware was all switched off, his body dull.

Speaker stood beside him, trying not to cry.

"Communicate with someone in the Military wing," ordered Rhododendron, flatly. The technomancer in the corner stood to attention to show that she had heard. "Ask them to free Ella. Suggest they follow his orders, if they haven't done so already. He was right."

Adora Ming slumped in her chair. She and Haja shared a cigarette, then another. Speaker glanced at it a few times but didn't ask for one.

The tech grunted and held their face, eyes closed tight in pain. "Apologies, I—It did something to our bioware. I—The Zetland is telling me that Apech's leader is here."

"What?" Rhododendron's voice regained some life. Rage, but life.

"Xar Kis, their commander. We have his info from the embassy on Apech. He's in the ship."

"You're absolutely sure?" Adora, standing up. "Where? We should have fucking known the worshippers would team up."

"Zetland can't be wrong. I'll show you him. They're here. Near the library."

Rhododendron's bicep flashed, and a panel slid out of the wall just like in Vard's room. Exactly like in Vard's room. He'd always been a fan. Pistols, seeking knives, spears. Adora grabbed a gun even before the emperor had the chance to take his own.

One by one Rhododendron's bioware began to blink, a faint whirling sound as he brought himself to light. He looked over the room, at each person individually. The techs, the black hands, the armed deodands. Silently, they waited for him.

"Well," he breathed. "I assume you're all coming with me?"

Speaker ran an odd gait to keep up with their twin's stride, knuckles white around a mechanical blade.

The sounds of the Zetland howled around them. Distant sirens shrieked for attention from technomancers probably dead. Explosions, bullets, the cries of irreal monsters making themselves known.

"Take the wall to your left," said the tech in their ranks. "Shortcut through to Green."

Rhododendron disappeared through the wall, a space in the Zetland's flesh marked by stripes at the holo wall's base. The rest followed, allowing its bloodstream to carry them faster as they marched.

When they emerged again they did so into the waste of battle. Hallway lights flickered. Strange masses writhed wormlike in the large, flat bulbs. Human bodies lay everywhere. There were patches of what seemed like tar dotted along the walls but it leached toward the dead, dragging itself along to congeal around them. It sounded like tongues clicking, it smelled like varnish.

At the far end of the corridor there was a boom and they span just in time to see a striped hare race past the junction, closely pursued by a small group of Greens carrying pots and pans. The sight was a comfort to them; perhaps people were winning. False hope. The cooks were not chasing. They were following, dragooned into holy service.

The highest-ranking Reds followed their emperor in the other direction.

"Why are we going such a long way?" asked Adora.

"I'm reading the Zetland," the tech said. "It's telling me which hallways are empty. But," she took a deep breath, clearly struggling.

"Stop, everybody stop. What's happening?" Rhododendron.

"Someone coming our way. Mid-ranking Green, but Zetland doesn't like him."

They heard his footsteps.

Rhododendron aimed, as did the others.

The man rounded the corner, greeting them with a pleasant smile. Still walking toward them.

"Stop there," Rhododendron ordered.

The man slowed, brows knotting, a hurt expression coming over his face. He held his hands up in a motion that said surrender but as he did so they saw that his palms were covered in fur.

"No," judged Rhododendron, opening fire.

The bullets hit, target assisted, inevitable. Three times in the chest. The man opened his mouth to scream but instead of a cry came the sound of a running stream, twigs cracking underfoot, an owl in the distance.

Everybody else opened fire, too.

When the man was nothing but shreds of immobile flesh Haja said: "Fuck."

"We don't have time for this shit." Rhododendron stepped over the ruined body. His comrades, normal sized, got their shoes wet.

26

Xar Kis recognized the Red emperor, saw himself recognized in turn. It was Xar's bearing, not his face, which gave him away as Apech's commander.

Xar shouted orders not to attack. He had spotted Speaker to Rhododendron's side.

The two leaders looked at each other, each reveling in his own certainty. Rhododendron had a gun. Xar had a god.

Neither spoke.

Adora couldn't take it any longer. Voice hard she growled, "Where is Mina? What did you do to her?"

Xar broke eye contact with Rhododendron, puzzled. "Who the hell is—Oh. Oh my. You look just like her."

"Don't you dare. Don't you dare taunt me."

"I haven't done anything to her," Xar replied, raising his voice into an infuriatingly honeyed tone of amiable reasonability. "She's around here somewhere, leading some of my troops. There's nothing stopping you from turning around and going to her."

Haja said, "Huh?"

Rhododendron glanced briefly at Adora then turned back to Xar. "Shut up."

"You don't believe me?" Xar laughed, looking around at his warriors. They grinned along with the joke. "Why do none of you people ever see it coming with that woman? Isn't it so obvious? This was almost entirely her idea."

"What are you saying?" Adora. She was crying. She sounded hopeful.

"Ignore him. He's just saying anything, stalling," Rhododendron snapped. "I've had enough."

He fired. Xar smiled, looking down at the place where his chest had opted not to be. "My god won't let you kill me, Your Highness."

Rhododendron kept firing. The others joined in.

After a few seconds of this there was another silence. The Crysthians looked to Rhododendron for help. He did not take his eyes off Xar.

"Although I am somewhat concerned that it can't do this all night long," Xar said, then turned to his soldiers, "Go on, be careful."

The Apechi flew forward. Xar was certain that they would take over the Zetland but not that they would manage to secure the stewards and officers. None of his soldiers would kill black hands and didn't dare even get close to Speaker, leaving them and their brother a lone island in the middle of the confrontation.

"Give me that knife," muttered Rhododendron.

Speaker thrust it over.

Rhododendron slipped his thumb over the part of the knife's handle that would deactivate its target assistance.

Speaker turned to look at Xar Kis, Crysth's undoer in the flesh. The man was watching them, not Rhododendron, a half-smile on his face. As Speaker watched him back, the smile turned into a leer and the eyes seemed to shift. Something was happening to the man's face that only Speaker with the god's infected vision could see. He appeared animal. In motion. His skin flickering between scale and skin. Speaker screamed, ran.

"No!" Xar yelled after them, grimacing in frustration at Rhododendron in his way.

The Red emperor stood a baffled tower of glowing skin, realizing that his enemy was looking past him. "Fucking fight me!" Petulant.

Xar really looked at him, then. As a foe rather than an obstacle. He believed that he could defeat him but that it would take time, which he did not have. He could not lose the steward in the maze of an unfamiliar palace, he could not allow Speaker to get themself killed by one of the demented halfgods stalking the ship.

The emperor was huge, metal, angry.

"Stay and die with your people," Xar suggested. "That would be the honorable thing to do, wouldn't it?"

Rhododendron's face showed confusion, disbelief.

Xar made a break for it, lurching to the emperor's left.

Rhododendron caught him. Massive steel fist, right in the sternum. Xar fell and rolled, springing out of the way on all fours to dodge past Rhododendron and run.

Both men were shocked by the other's strength. Xar had fought people with bioware before but never like that. For his part Rhododendron had expected the unaltered man to be far more squidgy. His fist hurt.

Now Xar found himself both chasing Speaker and fleeing Rhododendron. He was actually scared. This might have excited him in another circumstance; he had not felt real fear for decades. He could hear the emperor's footsteps slamming behind him.

Speaker's high-heeled boots were slowing them down. They skidded around a corner, thudded into a wall, saw that the enemy commander was chasing them. They screamed again, falling onto their hands before getting enough friction to start running. Frantically they searched the walls for a stripe, the slight variation in color which would tell them they could use it to get into the machine and disappear. Xar was gaining on them.

"Aaaah!" Speaker repeated themself as Xar became unavoidably close, swept them out of the air with an arm around their waist. The movement was agonizing, Xar had adjusted his physical expectations following contact with Rhododendron and nearly broke Speaker's ribs.

Gasping, Speaker was turned around to face their brother, cold tip of a sharpened railway spike to their throat. "Stop there," said Xar. "Stop."

Rhododendron pinged his eyes between Speaker and Xar, wondering whether or not he cared. He raised the knife in his hand.

"You will hit your steward."

Speaker whimpered.

"This is a seeking knife." Rhododendron's thumb slipped up the blade. "It will slit your throat without any effort from me."

"And my last act will be murder."

"We're all dead anyway." The emperor released his knife.

Speaker heard Xar hiss the word *shit* in their ear before he pushed them unharmed onto the floor. Xar raised his railway spike and fenced with the little knife. It reorientated itself after each deflection and accelerated back toward him like a deadly weathervane.

Still saying *shit, shit, shit*, Xar dueled with the floating blade. He was faster now that it had expended its initial acceleration, but it was relentless and small. Glancing again and again from the spike.

Rhododendron ignored Speaker. He didn't have long until the blade ran out of power. He threw himself at the invader, trying to knock him down, hold him still for the knife to do its work. They fell to the floor together, Rhododendron on top, crushing Xar's chest.

The seeking knife collapsed to the ground. Rhododendron snarled and grabbed it, allowing Xar to extend a protective arm over his head before the blade came down hard. They struggled—the knife's edge a creeping descent toward Xar's face, the spittle and sweat of Rhododendron's effort dripping into his gasping mouth.

"Ha," the emperor panted, spotting Xar's other hand reaching out desperately for the railway spike. "Speaker!" he yelled, "Speaker! Get . . . the . . . get the fucking . . . spike!"

Speaker stared, frozen. Listened to the piercing scream as Rhododendron sank his knife into the commander's eye.

Then Speaker saw the railway spike emerge bloody tipped from between their brother's shoulder blades.

Xar kicked the emperor's stomach, pushing him away. He staggered to his feet. With his one remaining eye he looked at Speaker, back to Rhododendron. Saw the emperor begin to stand.

Xar flinched from Rhododendron, holding his face. Eye destroyed. Blood leaking between his fingers. He was panicking. In his state of panic the god's assistance was a hindrance. It was showing him visions, trying to force him to act but just confusing him further. He couldn't see. He didn't feel like he could take his hand from his eye. He couldn't breathe. He lurched through the hallway, away from Rhododendron, looking for air.

Speaker cringed past Xar to help their brother, who held up a hand to keep them back. "No," he said, "I survived."

Speaker stopped. This was demonstrably untrue. Rhododendron's lights glitched, blood poured. He wasn't designed to fight. He leaked acid. He twitched.

"Rho—"

"No. Not like this." The giant man slumped down the wall, pulled himself back up. "He hasn't killed me."

"You're going to be okay." Tears rolled down Speaker's face.

"Am not. But it won't be him that killed me," he croaked. "He hasn't killed me."

Rhododendron turned, staggered across the hallway. Toward the library door.

"Where are you—sit down. Please. Please."

OUT OF ORDER, said the library.

"Where are you going?" sobbed Speaker. "Stay with me."

"No. It won't be him that killed me." Rhododendron swiped the back of his hand on the door. It complained once more that it was *OUT OF ORDER*, but it had no choice but to obey the emperor's hand.

The sound of Vard's deathly humming emerged tuneless from the depths of the room.

"Please," Speaker wailed, not daring to enter, watching Rhododendron collapse toward a table stacked with books.

The Red emperor's flashing, bloodied hands fell onto a paperback. He flipped open the cover and began ripping out its pages.

Vard's humming grew louder as the door slid shut.

OUT OF ORDER.

Speaker slid down the wall, clasping their knees, near choking on sobs wrenched from their bruised ribs. They rocked themself, chin shaking. They could taste snot and blood.

Something began to crackle to their left. They looked, blinking, wiping their face on their sleeve and clambering upright.

A sparkling stream of purple glitter poured toward them, behaving like smoke but lying perfectly flat a few feet from the floor.

"Stop it!" Speaker shrieked at the sparklefog and then turned to run. Retracing their steps, back toward the holo wall, back to the Red control wing.

Speaker felt worse as the sirens faded behind them—as the event descended from something that was happening to something that had happened. They kept running, even though the Red hallways seemed clear.

The control room. That's where it had started so that's where Speaker was going. To return, to hide.

They swiped their arm over the door and collapsed inside. A few black hands were still at the table, too old to keep up with the rest.

Speaker grasped the back of a chair and let tears fall onto the golden patterns of their fingers.

Silence while the steward wept.

"Rhododendron's gone."

No response.

"Do you hear me?" Speaker yelled, anger seeming an excellent replacement for loss. "Say something!"

Speaker looked up, seeing for the first time. The three figures slumped in their chairs, heads lolled.

A jolt through Speaker's heart. "Hello?"

The dead figures did not respond.

Speaker backed away, eyes darting around the room, looking for the danger.

"Hello?!" again. Pleading.

And then they saw the thing outside. A long, pointed snout. Jagged teeth resting together against the glass as it pressed its eye green and unblinking to the window.

Speaker screamed, ramming their wrist against the wall, fumbling to open the door.

They shot down the hallway. No longer knowing where they were going. Feet carrying them automatically back to their apartment. They were too terrified to notice that their door was already open.

They tore through the air, smashed their face into a freestanding fireplace. Someone had tripped them. They screamed again, bleeding, nose broken.

"Close the door!" came a woman's voice from within the room. Whoever had been waiting behind it obeyed.

Speaker stayed on the floor, rolled onto their back. Sniveling.

"You have to be joking." The woman's face surfaced into Speaker's vision overhead, looking down into their face with amused disbelief. "What were you going to do? Hide under your bed?"

Speaker choked, relieved. They were being ridiculed in the accent particular to Crysth's capital city—normality was restored.

"Help me," they ordered, reaching out to her.

The woman laughed.

Scowling, Speaker sat upright, squinting over their nose to look at her properly. "Adora? How—No." Something dawned. "Wilhelmina Ming?"

"No," she whispered. "Just Ming."

27

"I'm so sorry about all this," Speaker said.

"I don't want your apologies you turncoat fuckface, fuck! Let me out!" Ella commanded.

"I can't. I'm so sorry. You know I can't."

"Darling, have you lost your *mind*?" Ella rattled his chains as he raged. "Let me out! Let me out!"

"Please don't yell," Speaker entreated him, holding a bottle of sparkling Muhr white and two glasses. "It was so hard to convince Xar to let me in here." They watched sadly as Ella ranted, thrashing around the beam he'd been attached to. When he seemed to tire of this, Speaker said, "Look. Do you want a glass of this or not? I brought it specially. I've been saving it."

After a few dry sobs Ella replied, "Yes, for gods' sake. Godsdammit. Fuck you!"

Speaker nodded in dull acceptance of the fuck and set both glasses down.

Pop. They poured, then produced a metal straw from their inside pocket.

"You cannot be serious!"

"I can't untie your hands. Would you rather I held it to your lips?"

"No! Fucking give me that."

Speaker darted forward, placed down the glass, backed away.

Ella drained his glass then glared another into existence.

"Isn't it delicious?" Speaker said.

"You know damn well it is."

"Tastes just like cream."

"Yes." Ella set his jaw. "With a hint of coffee."

"Right? So complex."

"Shut the fuck up."

"Oh, Ella."

A silence. Then, "You look well." Accusingly.

"Thank you. No. I mean. . ." Speaker grasped for words, found none. "I'm a prisoner too, you know!"

"No you aren't!"

"Have you any idea how hard it was to hide this bottle from . . . *them*?"

"I'm chained to a beam!"

"They tortured me for weeks!"

"And now you're their pet!"

Speaker sniffed, pulled themself together, poured more wine with a shaky hand. "I didn't have to come here, you know."

"Why did you? I won't absolve you."

"I don't need absolution, I need to warn you. They will hurt you. They won't kill you. U6-93 wants you alive, I don't know why. But they will really, really hurt you. Please behave. I truly believe they're insane."

"I would revel in it. I will not give in."

Speaker shook their head. "Please give in."

"Kill them."

"How?"

"Figure it out!"

"I am not a soldier, I am a steward."

"I thought you were a prisoner?"

"I—Yes. You know what I mean."

"Do *you*?!"

Speaker frowned, then turned their head slightly. "They're coming. We're going to see the prophet. Please, please behave."

"Oh fucking hell, the circus assembles!"

"Calm down, be good."

"Be good?!"

"They are evil people!" whispered Speaker, rushing over to pour Ella one last glass before opening the door.

"There he is!" Xar grinned, striding in. "See? I got him."

"I didn't doubt that it was him," Ming said.

"Well, anyway."

Ella glowered at them.

"Oh don't look at me like that," Xar scolded. "Haven't you been bored? Haven't you felt cooped up in your little rebellion? It'll all be over soon."

"What the hell does that mean?" Ella asked.

"Nobody knows!" Xar replied, jolly. "But let's find out shall we?" His guards set about unfastening Ella's chains.

28

"And again, I see you." The translator spoke as batcardinal murmured into it. Ming stepped down from the ship, hand enveloped in his silver fingers. "Although I confess myself to have been concerned. It took you some time."

"There was," Xar interjected, "a god made of petals which kept turning people's body hair into petals and then convincing them to throw themselves off the balconies." The batcardinal looked about to speak so Xar raised his voice. "One day I woke up and there were crabs in the drinking water. Tiny crabs. So many tiny tiny crabs."

"So you met the god of crabs." U6-93 smiled. "In a world which tends to carcinization, is that not a useful friend to have?"

No idea what she was talking about, Xar grinned. "I am very happy to be back."

"And I to have you back. We have been thinking a great deal about our new alliance. Much to be discussed, much to be planned. I'm sorry the halfgod army caused so much pain for you."

The Ma delegation turned to watch as Ella was brought struggling out of the ship.

"Oh knock it off," Xar called to him. "What are you going to do?"

Batcardinal laughed and then said, "Oh?" as Speaker stepped gingerly down onto the roof.

"I would introduce you but you have already met," Ming offered. "Speaker, you know Dash and Fivepoint."

"I have had the pleasure of their acquaintance but under different circumstances." They held out their hand to grasp the prophet's. Ella screamed beneath his gag.

The prophet said, "I am happier than you can know to see you in this condition in these circumstances now. And though it may be uncouth, and it may lower the tone of our new meeting, I must say to you how deeply, truly sorry I am about your brother. I did try to reason with him. I swear to you that."

"Stabbed out my eye," Xar.

"Is that what happened?" batcardinal asked. "I assume you haven't had the time to build a replacement, rather than that Crysth does not have the capability?"

"I find it handsome," Ming.

"We shall have to hear this tale of your ocular halfening another time," the prophet said. By now they were all walking together across the cathedral's landing pad. "I'm sure you are as eager as we to proceed with this ritual."

At the word "ritual," Speaker's face did something strange. They still didn't know what was happening, but they decided to behave as if they did.

"My condolences about your cathedral," Ming nodded to the truncated building. "We did not see that coming. I hope damages were minimal."

U6-93 laughed. "Isn't Avon Stal marvelous? What a thing to have done."

The observatory doors opened as they neared. The rest of the cardinals were inside, as was Lucille.

"Finally!" he called. "We were beginning to worry." He looked over the gathering and said, "Speaker. Ella."

Ella began to thrash more against his guards at the sight of Lucille.

At shin height, one of Ma's outposts said: "Mrow."

Xar picked her up. "Hello little sweetie. Aren't you the sweetest? Don't we have a nice little empire. Crysth-Ma. You like Crysth-Ma?"

"Ma-Crysth," corrected batcardinal.

"Ma-Crysth?" Speaker, unbelieving.

"Of course." Ming, whispering low as if to shush a child. "What did you think was going to happen?"

"We've been wondering what to call the people of Ma-Crysth," said Lucille, standing a few feet in front of Ella and staring straight at him. "Ma-Crysthians?"

"Ma-Crysthi?" Batcardinal.

"Ma-Crysthmites." The prophet.

"It's too soon to be thinking in these terms. We must do this slowly, carefully," Ming reasoned.

"Ma-Crysthons." Xar.

"Ma-Crysthats?" Lucille.

"You can't just suddenly tell billions of people they're Ma-Crysthats," Ming said, her voice rising.

"Can we tell them they're Ma-Crysthi?" batcardinal asked.

"No you—You're all annoying me on purpose. We have a ritual to perform."

"*We* have a ritual to perform," batcardinal corrected. "You will watch. Lucille, leave him alone!"

They all looked in the direction of batcardinal's shouting. Lucille was tapping his robotic finger on Ella's forehead. He withdrew it with a "Sorry."

"Now," began the prophet, "we know we do not know what is about to happen. But we can make one assumption based on last time." She looked gravely between the two stewards. "We are likely going to lose one of you."

"What?" Speaker squealed.

Ella went quiet, stopped struggling.

"It's up to Speaker," said Ming. "Speaker will decide."

"What, what will I decide?"

The prophet strolled over to hold Speaker's hand, speaking to them softly. "We must commune with the god that has made your body its home. We must do this to know what it does. For the good of the future, yes? We cannot control or worship or love what we do not know."

"What, commune how?"

"We need both of you," she said, "but I believe that only one will remain. Last time we tried, you see. Only one remained."

The room changed. An electric buzzing. Low, quiet.

Ming's heart thudding in her butchered chest. "It's already here."

Ma's tail curled lovingly around Xar's arm. The body purred.

"It is." Batcardinal's voice barely a breath.

"This is what it wants." The prophet, to Speaker. "The two stewards it requested from us. The two of you together. We do not know but we do believe that one of you will today be made a martyr for our empire. I believe I can direct this. Shall the sacrifice be yours?"

"I . . . I can't—"

"You will be the one to decide, Speaker," Ming said. "You are the Red steward, after all."

"I am? Who is—Who is the emperor?"

"Ming, of course." Xar, suddenly by Speaker's side. "Time to start being a bit faster on the uptake."

Ella screamed beneath his gag. With a frown the prophet said, "Will we hear what the Military man has to say? I believe we should." She did it herself, stalked over to him and disengaged the metal gag so gently with her silver fingers that for a moment Ella forgot to shriek.

When he regained himself, he yelled, "You are not the Red emperor, and you are not the Red steward! You are all traitors. You are not Rhododendron!"

"Nobody is Rhododendron," said Ming.

"That's true," Xar agreed. "We live in a world devoid of Rhododendrons. Is that all you have to say?"

"You're all evil! You're just spacefreaks! You're nothing! None of this will come to anything! You've destroyed something beautiful for nothing! Kill me, you sick fucks, I don't want to live to see a world of your design! You've fucked it all up! It's all fucked!"

"Well, Speaker?" Ming asked.

Trembling. Eyes on the floor. Tears spilling, ruining makeup. Speaker nodded.

"Remember me, you sad, sick little fuck! Remember me when this all falls the fuck down on your evil spacefreak head!"

"What was that, Speaker?" Ming asked again. "You're choosing Ella?"

"Yes. I . . . I'm so sorry. I'm so sorry."

"Coward! Traitor!"

The prophet reapplied the mechanism to Ella's face as tenderly as she had removed it. "Well," she said.

"Well done, Speaker," Ming said. "We're going to need you on the altar, next to Ella."

"Would you like to be rendered unconscious?" the batcardinal asked Speaker, pushing a needle into Ella's neck. Ella slumped in the Apechi guards' grasp.

"Ah, ah . . . No . . . I . . . No."

"It will hurt," Xar said.

"I deserve it."

The Apechi god's thrum was growing louder.

"I confess myself alarmed by the Apechi deity's already palpable excitement. It wants this very badly." Batcardinal.

"Ma is not alarmed." The prophet.

Batcardinal nodded unhappily as he removed Ella's gag and bonds. He could feel Ma's pleasure, irreal though it was. He could not argue with that. "Positions," he said, and the cardinals were at the room's perimeter.

The prophet placed her hands onto Speaker's shoulders and applied pressure until they were lying down beside Ella, looking up into her daggertooth smile. "Are you excited to find out what's happening?" she asked.

Descending into sobbing incredulousness Speaker answered, "No."

She laughed.

Electricity crackled as batcardinal opened a tiny velvet case which held the Apechi deity's needle and thread. He lacked the prophet's abandon, her wild curiosity, but even he felt the exhilaration of the moment. It was unavoidable. The room was alive, explosive, kinetic.

The prophet sank the needle into Speaker's forearm. They cried out, fell silent.

What Speaker felt next was the closest the untrained can know to nothingness. A death, a disappearance. A moment of perfect absence, a complete lack of self. A world but nobody through which to know it. It was beautiful. It was like being saved.

But then there was birth. Something pulling them sick back into time. And there were so many times, dragging on and intertwining and coming apart again. Later Speaker would swear they were screaming but there was no sound, no movement. They were screaming in resistance. They did not want to come back, back from that perfect nowhere.

Ella's eyes shot open.

The prophet staggered backward, dropping the needle. The cardinals stopped their chanting, bat rushed forward to her.

Speaker groaned, gasped, wailed at the pain in their arm. Looked down to see the thick string pulling at their flesh, binding them to Ella—who was sitting upright.

"Agh," he groaned, raising his untouched left arm, flexing his fingers. The arm trembled.

Apechi guards stepped forward to put Ella down again but the prophet called out and they stopped. "It's not him," she said. "There's someone, there's someone else—"

"What the fuck." Xar.

Ming held Xar's sleeve.

Ma the cat leapt from Xar's arms. It demanded to be lifted to the altar. Ella groaned again, voice gravelly and strange.

"*Yes,*" he said, "*yes.*" He was speaking Apechi.

"What the fuck?" Xar.

"What's happening?" Lucille.

"He's speaking Apechi. Can Ella speak Apechi? Is it—is it the god, is it talking to us?" Ming said, with a panic in her voice.

"*Shut . . .*" slurred Ella, "*shut up.*"

Believing that god had just told her to shut up, Ming did so.

Ella began to pull away, ripping stitches, detaching. Speaker wailed and tried to grab his hand, bring the arm back down. Ma bit happily at their bloody wrists.

"Get this thing off me." Ella's voice, speaking in Crysthian but with a heavy Apechi accent.

After a moment of hesitation, it was Xar who moved forward first, pulling a knife out of Ming's belt and undoing the thread. Batcardinal came to help.

Freed, Speaker heaved away. Lucille caught them and helped them to the floor.

"It's okay, it's okay," Lucille was saying. "You're alright." Speaker seemed to disagree.

"Ella?" Xar snapped his fingers in front of Ella's face. He was clearly struggling to focus.

"Is that Farön Kis's son?" Ella whispered.

Dawn broke in Ming's mind. The promise of realization but not yet its fact—there was only one person she had ever heard refer to Xar Kis as if he were an incompetent upstart but this could not be that person. He was dead, he had been killed on Apech, and his corpse eaten by the god he controlled. "Xar," she said, "the priest."

"What is happening here?" Batcardinal.

Ella staggered off the altar, managing to remain upright by holding himself against it. He found the prophet and steadily lowered his head in her direction. He was bowing. "Thank you," he said. "Your skill is . . . magnificent. I have felt none like it before."

"I see," breathed Xar. "It is you. I thought you were ate."

Ella's head shot around to face Xar. He said, "No I was not *ate,* you fool, I was subsumed. I became one with our god that I might preserve myself, control it. Control *you.* I find myself shocked that you managed to get us here even with my holy guidance." He stopped to breathe deeply, rasping. "I am in the body of the Military steward, yes?"

"Yes, yes," hurried Ming.

"I better be. If I'm that Red one I will kill you all."

"You are within the body of the Military steward," Lucille said, translating for U6-93. "But what are you?"

"I am . . . the last priest of Apech. No. In this new world, I am the first priest of Apech. I have been waiting."

U6-93 grinned, teeth shining. "You are the one who spoke to me. You . . . are a prophet. Your control is . . . You are the one holding the Apechi deity. You are why it is so precise. Your control is unbelievable." Her heart thumped with joy. This was the moment in which she discovered that it wasn't just her who could manipulate the unreal, she wasn't an anomaly. Here was another with her ability and so she was not a freak, she was a *type.* If there can be two there can be many more, there is hope that the people of Ma will be safe from the god after her death.

"And yours," he said. "And yours, too."

Speaker's eyes appeared over the edge of the altar, looking to Ella's animated body.

Batcardinal snapped his fingers for someone to tend not-Ella's arm.

"You're controlling the god," Speaker said, voice tiny. "You're the one who did all this? You've been directing everything, all this time?"

"What?" Ella's voice scoffed. He jerked his chin over to Kis and Ming. "You didn't think it was those two, did you?"

29

Xar's lowered brow formed a dark horizon, upside down. His pupil travelling left and right beneath it. Unblinking. Watching Ella pace.

"It isn't time that my god controls," Ella was saying, a translator wound around his ear. "It is deconstruction."

Ma's clergy were wild with delight. A new god, a new world. No borders no boundaries all freedom. A universe to course through arm in arm, two prophets at their helm. They observed him as students rapt to a master's attention. U6-93 could barely sit still.

"How?" urged the batcardinal. "I need to know precisely, how?"

"My respect for your skill is great, but I suspect your method holds you back," responded Ella's voice, his accent wrong. "There is no such thing as precise, here. Not in our mundane terms. Your prophet knows this."

Batcardinal took this well, a shallow bowing of the head followed by: "Granted. As precisely as is available to us, perhaps? It will help me, and I know it will help the rest of the clergy. We are to become a dual theocracy; we must know what you are."

"Deconstruction," snapped the man who was not Ella, stopping suddenly and turning to face the batcardinal. "Not destruction. Constant remaking. Understand this first."

Speaker sat on the floor in front of Ming, leaning back against her legs. She was ecstatic. Here was the man who had promised her the god's power, here she was having done everything he asked of her and more. There was nothing left in her way. Her eyes were wide with love and she smiled beneath her mask. Speaker's hair glittered between her fingers as she played with its lengths.

"The world in our theology is a vulnerable thing," continued Ella. "Always made and undone. Reconstructed every second."

"You are being literal?" Batcardinal.

Ella stopped again, flexed his neck.

Exhausted though Speaker was, they could not help but stare at the abomination of Ella's body. The thing occupying it was wholly not him. Gone was any of Ella's round, theatrical extravagance—the bouncing pleasure of his gait, the singsong delight of his voice. This new thing was loping yet stilted, stingy with its movements. Before he lost his own body the Apechi priest had been much older than Ella, and that was obvious. An austerity in the gaze, a low certainty in the voice. He was taking a beautiful thing and making it dangerous, ugly. The effect kept reminding Speaker of Avon Stal—an object frighteningly unlike the way it looked.

But what bothered Speaker most of all about the sight of Ella so magnificently possessed was the suspicion that Ella was not dead. Neither dead nor stuck in limbo—not trapped beside the Apechi imposter in his own body but back *there*. In the nothing. The perfect nothing. What bothered Speaker most of all was the thought that they had made the wrong choice when they decided not to sacrifice themself instead.

"I do not know," replied Ella, to the delight of the prophet. "I have seen what my god sees, but how am I to know whether literality exists in its eyes? It sees a world constantly obliterated. Every time a decision is made, a world is destroyed. An ocean of possibilities lost. But it remembers them. No. Listen to me here. I do not know whether it remembers them, or they are real. But it can access them."

"We see things that were supposed to have happened, but won't anymore, and can make them happen anyway," Xar, unexpectedly.

Ella turned to appraise him and said, "Yes. That is a useful way to think of it. But not always true."

"You've never said that before." Ming, looking at Xar.

"I never thought of it like different worlds before. It seems almost obvious now. My body can remember everything it could have been."

"Yes," hissed Ella, "good boy."

"The universe is destroyed and remade every time something changes. Your god can see all the destroyed universes," said the prophet. "Is this correct?"

"Perhaps. Either these places of different possibilities truly exist and it can access them, thereby granting us access to them also, or these places do not exist but the god has a *construct* of them. An idea or a memory of what they could have been. And these constructs, holy as they are, are so powerful as to be actionable."

"*Real are the dreams of gods.*" Speaker, murmuring.

"What?" Ming.

"Keats. Earth-era literature."

"Yes!" she whispered, "I told you. Humanity has always known. This is the way. Even back then when we didn't know anything. This is right. This is right."

"How far into the future can you see?" the prophet asked.

"I cannot. I can see calculations. Designs. This is what leads me to believe that these other worlds or universes as you put it do not truly exist. They are shades, ideas." He looked at Xar. "Xar Kis is stronger than anyone could be because he can use all of that potentiality at the same time. All the different ideas about how things could have been. Sometimes, his body can remember having evolved differently. He can access possibilities that he was a different creature. With true mastery . . . I do not know what we will be capable of. But we will together find out."

Ming beamed.

"Can you control Crysth's machinery?" Lucille asked.

"With ease. I will train more priests to do the same. Perhaps even Crysth's 'technomancers' can be tutored in the ecclesiastical arts."

Speaker finally allowed themself to close their eyes.

30

Ming sat cross-legged on the sofa in her new apartment. Ella stood with his back to her, gazing into a mirror, repeating words as she said them.

"Initiate. Totalitarian. Titillate. Tantrum," she said.

"Initi—"

"No. Initi. Init-iate," she spat the sound. "Tuh. Tee. Ta."

"Tuh. Tee. Da."

"Almost. It's like the T in *tama*, I don't understand how you can pronounce it at the beginning of a word but not the middle."

"This is neither my language nor my tongue," he growled, lowering his eyes to look at her in the glass. His accent had not yet improved—he could not pretend to be Ella in public until it had.

"We're going to have to think of an excuse. A reason that conversion to theism might have messed with your tongue."

"No. If they think him physically altered, they will be afraid."

"Well then. You're also going to have to start calling everyone darling."

The priest sneered with Ella's mouth. "Darling?"

"It's what he did. Everyone was 'darling.' An affectation."

"Darling."

"Sorry."

He turned to look at her face rather than its reflection. Mangled meat with an expression of hopefulness, of trust. "And you," he said, "what will be your first action as Red emperor?"

She swallowed. "Other than restoring Crysth to normality? I supposed that . . . I supposed that making me like you would be—"

"No."

She paused, thoughts emptying. "What?"

"I know what you want. I know you want to be touched by the blessing of our god. I remember promising it to you and at one point I believed I would fulfill that promise but can no longer. You are now too important."

"Wh . . . what do you mean?" She was beginning to panic. She could feel her face growing hot. Sweat prickling under the metal torso of her suit.

"You cannot be one of us," he pronounced, slowly. "How was that, my accent?"

"I . . . why? What are you saying to me?"

"Stay calm. Calm down or I will not speak to you."

"I am calm!" she shrieked.

"No."

"I am calm," she repeated.

"You are *tama*," he said. "At one point it wouldn't have mattered. I would have let it into you, I would have let it strip you of your foul uncomplicated mind and I would have watched quite happily as you became the base, thoughtless filth that you were born to be. But no more."

"No. No. What do you mean? It can't—"

"The god does not want you. It would tear through you. You have nothing for it."

"You're wrong. You have to be wrong. I did all this."

He grinned. "It does not matter. An adult cannot survive metamorphosis. You have known this all along. You deluded yourself into thinking that you would be an exception, that your good behavior would make it soften, bend the rules. My god does not care. You are nothing to it. This is not my problem."

"No . . . I . . . Speaker lived."

"Speaker lived because I was inside them. In control."

"Well, well, get back in!"

The grin remained as he said, "No. You are parasitic. But you are so adept a parasite that I cannot allow my god to hollow you out. You are so adept in fact that the host cannot live without you. You will be the Red emperor. You will sit on that throne and you will perform for me. That is your role."

"Please, no. I did everything right . . . No."

"Yes," he hissed, with obvious delight. "You will."

Her sobs ripped the seams between her rib cage and her new, plastic skin. She screamed in pain and heaved again with the horror of loss. It pulled into her. She could not think it, so grotesque so impossible so evil it was that she felt herself newly realizing it every moment, unable to keep it stable in her mind. Impossible. Impossible. Happening.

"Pull yourself together. They are coming. Xar Kis does not need to know what you really are. It would disgust him."

The door swung open. Speaker came in first, chattering with excitement, flatscreen in hand. "We've reestablished contact with almost everyone at this point. We will be back on Crysth in a few months but that is not wasted time—we can make valuable stopping points on the way and reassure everyone that Crysth is functioning as usual."

"I will not be comfortable saying that until we have located Daksha," Kis replied. "She's still out there somewhere."

"Yes. We must locate Daksha and your lost general," Ella growled. "They could be a problem." Darkly he added, "Darlings."

"Ha!" laughed Speaker, "You'll have to do his hand movements too, flouncy fingers like this. And he only drinks sparkling wine."

"I am not doing flouncy fingers. What the hell is sparkling wine?"

Xar noticed Ming, her hands over her face, her body quaking. "Ming?"

She shook her head, waved him away.

He strode over, kneeling in front of her. "What's wrong? We've won. It's ours, we have everything."

Her teeth chattered in her ruined mouth. Her voice shook. Her lips tore as she dragged them into a smile and said: "I'm just so happy."